The Ghosts of Kerfol

The Ghosts of Kerfol

꙳ DEBORAH NOYES ꙳

CANDLEWICK PRESS

Copyright © 2008 by Deborah Noyes

First paperback edition 2010

The Library of Congress has cataloged the hardcover edition as follows:

Noyes, Deborah.
The ghosts of Kerfol / Deborah Noyes. — 1st ed.
p.   cm.
Summary: Over the centuries, the inhabitants of author Edith Wharton's fictional mansion, Kerfol, are haunted by the ghosts of dead dogs, fractured relationships, and the taste of bitter revenge.
ISBN 978-0-7636-3000-3 (hardcover)
[1. Haunted houses—Fiction. 2. Ghosts—Fiction.
3. Supernatural Fiction.]   I. Title.
PZ7.N96157Gh 2008
[Fic]—dc22   2007051884

ISBN 978-0-7636-4825-1 (paperback)

10 11 12 13 14 15 RRC 10 9 8 7 6 5 4 3 2 1

Printed in Crawfordsville, IN, U.S.A.

This book was typeset in Centaur.

Candlewick Press
99 Dover Street
Somerville, Massachusetts 02144

visit us at www.candlewick.com

For Liz and Amy

Contents

Hunger Moon

1613

WHEN THE COACH SET ME DOWN before that avenue of trees—straight and stern with cicadas screaming in the tall branches—I saw no welcome for a starved brat missing her mama.

At the end of the avenue, past a clearing where many lanes met, past an iron gate and two vast gardens where all manner of herbs and flowers hunkered, still and sweet-smelling in the sloping shadows, stood the gray mass of the château, flanked by towers. A moat circled it, gleaming darkly. A wide sweep of steps led up to the entrance.

My oldest cousin, Étienne, who later became a trapper in the New World, had once been a potboy in a château like this. Serfs were sent each night, he said, to stamp on the bullfrogs in the moat so the master could sleep. Drawing near, I imagined the wet crunch of small bodies, torches reflecting in rank water, and

I prayed to the Virgin that I would not be called upon to smash frogs.

The front door was high like a church's. I longed for the hearth light within, for soup and a bit of crust, but the meaty, sullen maid would not open it.

"Milady's asleep," she scolded through a crack, "and I have no instructions for you. The stable's in the courtyard out back. Don't blunder into the men's quarters next door; it's the stone building you want. You'll find straw in the empty stall." She slapped shut the door and then opened it again. "Come to the kitchen at sunup."

I ventured out back and ducked under the low arched doorway of the stable, feeling my way through the dark as snuffling horses reached out to me. Gripped by the profound silence of the manor, I slept the fitful sleep of a criminal that night, my stomach hollow as a hive when all but one angry wasp has left it. I might have known then that Kerfol was a neglectful house, preoccupied with its woes.

The dull prongs of a pitchfork woke me.

"Look here," a voice teased. "I've found a leg in the straw. A fine-looking one, too. And a shoulder. What else?"

"Ack!" I complained. "Don't!"

Up I rolled onto my knees to find a lanky boy. I saw at once with grave alarm that his lashes were a bleached shade of copper, like snow where the hawk has hunted, and his hair was a bolder shade of the same. Grand-mère, who had devoted herself to scaring children witless, fancied tales of the *loup-garou*, an unfortunate human who'd lapped water from the left paw print of a wolf. When the moon swelled, he turned savage, though he had no wolf's tail because, the priests said, God did not permit the Devil or his instruments right form. Sometimes, too, the curse traveled in the blood. A beast in human form inherited hairy palms, a third finger longer than the second, and, yes, red hair. Here stood the very creature from my oldest nightmare, and I hadn't the sense to feel frightened. Not really. If this Red Boy was a werewolf, he was a pretty one.

"You'll be the new waiting woman, then." He spoke with a smiling accent, hazel eyes slipping to my breasts on the count of "woman" as if to prove the claim.

I crossed my arms.

He leaned back against the stall, and we regarded one another awhile.

At length, he set aside the pitchfork and reached down.

"First, promise you were *not* born on Christmas Eve," I said. According to Grand-mère, all werewolves were.

"I promise," he said solemnly.

"Whose promise is it?" I went on boldly. "Who offers his hand?"

"Youen, mademoiselle." He bowed, and I took the hand and let him heave me up. "The stable boy. The horses will speak for me." He let go almost clumsily, sweetly, stroking a mare in the stall beyond, which whinnied in answer. "There," he said. "You see?"

The clatter of hooves sounded on the gravel outside, and we both rallied, he to greet the rider and I to grope, blushing, in the hay for my clogs and hemp sack.

In the kitchen, the maid from the night before, whose name was Maria, informed me that it would be my domain only temporarily. Cook had hired me, but in the end, the château had more need in the bedchambers and laundry. "Tomorrow an upstairs woman named Guillemette will see to you," said Maria, who seemed less sullen in daylight. "But today we're all needed here."

The entire staff of Kerfol, it appeared, had been summoned to stage a feast for a Norman noble and his son. The horseman that morning had been the noble's servant, arrived to announce his master. The riding party would reach Kerfol by evening, he said, so the baron had set off at once to the hunt and sent his servants scurrying to shore and market for fish and produce.

Cook oversaw the excavation of dusty jars of vinegar, mustard, cinnamon, cloves, saffron, and ginger. She fetched from who knew where olive oil and pomegranates, oranges, lemons, figs, and plums. By noontide, pots were full and spits were turning, and I was henceforth tormented by smells.

I quick grew fond of the kitchen, and disappointment that I would be exiled from it, assigned elsewhere, must have shown on my face. Everything did in those days. Maria beat a round of dough, her bright eyes crinkling like an old woman's, though she couldn't have had more than three years over my sixteen, and said, "We're merry today, it's true, but we're always so before the public."

And?

"Never mind, now." She brushed flour off her hands. "Here, take over the bread making. I've too much else to do."

She showed me how to tend the great hearth and slip spongy loaves into the brick wells with a long-handled shovel. She drew out a golden loaf and flicked it with a fingernail, as if I'd never before baked bread. "Hear that? Nice and crisp. Stack them in that oak cupboard, and whatever you do, don't let the fire go out, or we'll have to send to the farmer's wife for coals. No time for that today."

Soon I'd exceeded my order of twenty loaves, swept up the flour, and resorted to thumbing through copies of *A New Booke of Cookery* and *The Accomplished Lady's Delight in Preserving, Physick, Beautifying, and Cookery*, though I learned their titles only a good deal later. The books' black type swam in my brain like minnows when the tide turns, but the pictures pleased me, almost as much as the smells that day.

My nose became a hound's, heroic in its efforts to identify and classify. Whenever someone with a friendly face went by with a pot or platter, my eyes begged, *What's in there?* One pock-faced runt even took pity, barking like a harassed innkeeper when he passed: "Shoulder of mutton with oysters," or "Venison pasty with cherries and crème."

Once the family and guests were served and the plates cleared, more and more sweet things passed and plagued me in my idleness: countess cakes and egg pie, apple cream and orange pudding. *How could all this be,* I thought stubbornly, *and not be mine?*

How indeed.

"You are thin enough," Maria said as if reading my mind, striding past with gingerbread and a pitcher of clotted cream. "But you'll get thinner."

"You're not so thin," I teased when she returned from the main dining room empty-handed.

"I take a lion's share of pride in the fact that I keep a woman's figure," she boasted, "on the scraps I'm fed." She thrust out her not insubstantial chest just as Youen entered with a cider cask on his shoulder. Once he'd passed, stony-faced, we covered our mouths, stooping, and laughed uproariously into our palms.

"I'm glad you've come," Maria said then, smoothing her apron, and for the first time since my parents had sold me into service, I was glad, too. I let my mind wander out after Youen and his copper-colored hair. I'd never seen such hair before, only heard about it in Grand-mère's stories.

Not ten minutes later, Maria's slap stung my knuckles. Worse yet, it made me drop the macaroon

I'd filched from a passing tray. The treat lay steaming an instant in the kitchen hay before a hen rushed out to peck at it. My mouth watered, and I looked away before my eyes did, too, thinking, Wasn't it a puzzle? I'd grown up among peasants, yet it took a great house to teach me hunger.

"*Where* are your wits?" she accused.

"I thought just a taste—" My voice sounded small in the bustle, a very different bustle from the one back home. Here all were quiet as they went about their chores, and they were skin and bones except Maria, every one. "There's so . . . much."

"So much?" Maria's brows arched. "And every crumb's accounted for. You risk worse than a whipping, stealing from the baron's pantry."

They were foolish words but rolled out of my mouth before I could stop them: "It was nothing."

Maria was our mother hen, our gossip in that house of horrors, our good captain, though I didn't know it then. On that day, my first at Kerfol, I thought her a scold. She peered close, astonished or nearsighted or both. "Here we call it *stealing*, Mooncalf. We take our meals when *he* wills it."

I looked down at my dusty clogs, picturing the flawless new pair Papa had crafted for me, the gift that came with his parting smile. *For you, Chicken. Lest you shame me in the baron's chapel on Sundays.* "Yes, I'll grant I'm distracted today." The shoes were safe in my hemp sack, together with spare bonnets and a feather from the little bird

Grand-mère had stolen from its mother's nest in spring: Percy, who sang in his cage of sticks and twine. Missing them, all of them, would be another sort of hunger. "Though I hope to grow wise soon," I added dutifully.

"Hear me, then." Maria leaned closer still, too close for my liking, and for the first time that day I really looked into her eyes. What I saw there surprised me, concealed in her otherwise brisk aspect. Was it terror? Sadness? I know not, but it cowed me. "Keep your hands to yourself," she warned, "and your eyes on me. Do as I do."

I held my breath, ashamed of my ignorance.

"Do only that."

I nodded, exhaling as she moved away.

Maria opened the pantry door and spat through it into the dust. "A taste," she mimicked. "Ha." She shut the door, and to soothe the mood between us, I opened it again, spat in my turn, and shrugged.

"You said to do as you do."

A smile bloomed on her stern face. "Good girl," Maria said, and tweaked my chin.

My first sight of Milady should have confirmed all.

She wasn't slight so much as wasted, over-lean and luminous like the nymph of a young beech tree with a head of crow's gloss. The black hair was pulled back severely from her face, pinned with elaborate lacquered combs for an exotic look. All told, she looked at the edge of health somehow — balanced, I would learn, on the blade of her own hunger.

When the mistress came into the kitchen, fanning herself with silk, Maria did a little mincing curtsey and dragged me over by the hand. "Here's Perrette, Milady, your new chambermaid. She arrived last evening, but too late to greet you."

The lady surveyed me, took my chin almost roughly — there was more strength in those slender hands than I might have guessed — moved my face this way and that, and her cool expression warmed. She set loose my jaw and held out her ringed hand. I stared in grateful, bovine fashion at the creamy knuckles.

"Kiss it," Maria hissed close to my ear, then straightened up to plead, "She's had no practice, Milady. Today is her first in service."

The mistress revoked the hand with a bemused smile, reaching out to brush stray hair from my eyes. "Pretty thing." Her voice was thin and absent, and she lowered it in a thrilling way, as if we had a secret. "Take your ease. I am happy today."

She turned to Maria. "Sire would have more cider for the table. Send Perrette. You and Cook may feed the others."

My stomach pitched as the lady glided away in a rustle of satin and Maria thrust a jug of cider at me, urging, "Don't put your arm over their plates while you pour."

Youen and several others were already gathering at the servants' table as I passed. Oddly, there were no dogs beneath in the straw, ready for what morsels might come. What French table had no dog under it? I wondered as that little group eyed me.

I was a spectacle, it would seem, poised at what felt to be the edge of fate on that threshold, frozen ridiculously to the floor. But I had to wait till my hand stopped shaking lest I spill. I peeked round and glimpsed the huge chimneypiece strung with firearms, bows, hunting horns, and antlers hooked with whips and leashes.

Sire had shouted orders from his horse that morning, so I recognized in the low, manly murmur out there my new master's voice, lamenting. With the harvest near, the women in his manor and village were waging a constant war on moles. *You are one of those women now,* I told myself. Breathing deep, I ducked in and was dazzled—as one who dives into fast-moving water is dazzled—by the roaring hearth fire reflected in pewter and green glass, copper and leather gilding. Every shelf was lined with fine things that glimmered. The sideboard groaned under cold heaps of lamb pie and homemade sausage, roast carp, plover, and wood pigeon: the greasy remains of the array that had crisscrossed under my nose all day.

I inched my way around the long table, pausing at each indifferent elbow as Sire and the visiting noble compared apple-planting methods. They spoke of manure, of scraping moss and cutting suckers, of whether ants were better repelled by pepper or by sand. They spoke of their pleasure in the ripening crop.

The party reclined in large cushioned oak chairs, with Sire at the head, and the only items left on the table were the saltcellar, spoons, wineglasses, and cider mugs. I poured carefully and well, my hand trembling only just.

"Now to mend the barrels, yes, Yves?" said the visiting noble, who went on to boast that he was a high priest of the Norman apple cult. It mustn't be so easy, he hinted, nor profitable, to plant the beauties in Brittany when Norman soil suited them better.

Even I knew the two patriarchs were sparring, and the others at the table held vague faces, sipping and smiling. Then a voice I hadn't heard before sounded. Strong, yet youthful, this voice had the gravity of an angel's. Not some silly cupid, I thought, but the sort that steps from behind a tree to cast its shadow o'er you while you toil in the fields, one of the fearsome archangels from Grand-mère's Bible tellings. What left his lips rang with prophecy, tender and merciful, but also fiercely irrefutable. The words themselves were playful, of little consequence—spoken with the air of one roused from boredom—but each left an echo.

He told how he had grown up hanging like a monkey from his father's apple trees. "I've traveled the world," he boasted, "but have loved no place better than my father's orchard in moonlight."

I stole a look at him in the shadows down the table and had to catch my breath, for he was staring straight at the mistress of the house while he spoke these sentimental words. "The trees," he said, "look like dancing girls then, their silvery hair thrown forward." It was the noble's son, I realized, Hervé de Lanrivain. It had to be. Besides Milady, there were no others under thirty-count in the room.

The silence fast grew oppressive, so I hastened to fill every mug as the noble cleared his throat, jesting that his impudent son would sooner soldier or spout poetry than govern or grow so much as a weed.

A strange new mood had seized the party, I realized, with Milady at its center. Blameless, yet blamed somehow, her eyes fixed firmly on ringed hands lying flat as submissive dogs on the table. The silence said so. "Why not walk your guests out among the apple trees then, husband?" she soothed. "Show them your pride."

Sire grunted in assent, and, following her suit, the gentlemen rose as one.

I think I did not take in air till I rounded the corner, and then with such incredulous gasping that every servant at the long kitchen table must have heard.

Mercy.

I'll never know what transpired in the orchard. Maria took me by the shoulders, guided me to a free chair, and the roiling energy at that crowded table absorbed me. "*Now,*" she said, "you may eat."

Cook spooned pottage with turnips into my bowl, grinning beneficently, and some two dozen servants mastered a smile at my expense.

Only this?

They did not linger long on my misfortune, and in spite of it, I ate gratefully. Everyone spoke at once, conspiring to educate me. "First, she'll try to make you her own handmaiden," one upstairs girl advised, "but he won't have it, and you'll end up in the laundry till she no longer pines for you. Then Sire will let you back in to change the beds again. But by this time, your hands are already ruined from the lye." The party laughed, and my face colored, though I didn't mind their attentions overmuch. There was comfort in the teasing, a hint of home.

Youen, who'd cleared his bowl and leaned back easily with an arm on his neighbor's chair, winked at me across the table. It was a brotherly wink as much as to say, *This will all make sense in time,* but it reminded me of our morning encounter in the barn. This time I winked back.

With a swift, secret smile, he stood and walked his plate to the washbasin.

The others continued to gossip over wooden bowls with Youen at the door keeping watch, and I learned that the baron and his wife were childless and without personal attendants. Sire trusted no one enough to be his *laquais,* Cook said. His cross-eyed farmer,

Symonette, was the closest he had to an attendant, and he'd suffer no cultured hands but his own to touch his wife, even a handmaiden's. Only unsmiling peasants like Guillemette were permitted to attend her, though the lady would have given much for a companion to sing and sketch with by the fireside.

Later, as we scrubbed the meat grease off the iron pots with sand, Maria said, "He's less given to gloomy silences since she came."

"Who?" My mind had strayed back to the Red Boy, Youen.

Maria went on as if she hadn't heard. "He's less harsh with his tenants. But I doubt *she's* happy."

I elbowed her out of her reverie. "Who will know?" I asked, dipping my finger into the dregs of a pudding.

Once more Maria reached out, though she did not slap my hand this time, only caught my wrist and held it fast. She leaned close and whispered, "The walls have eyes. They have ears, too. And don't forget it."

The eyes were his.

The ears were his.

The baron was of hard, squat build with a sharp silver beard. He was a great horseman and hunter, though like many wealthy nobles, he spent his days managing the estate, superintending the harvest, and holding court. When he could, he liked to tend his apple trees, Youen explained.

Though I knew few of the particulars of their marriage until later—at the trial toward which my whole young life now craned—I learned that sixty-seven-year-old Yves de Cornault, lord of the domain of Kerfol, had met young Anne de Barrigan of Douarnenez at Locronan the previous spring. A day later he'd sent his steward, and mules heaped with gifts. The following week Yves de Cornault announced to his vassals and tenants that he would marry Anne de Barrigan at All Saints' Day, which he did, with fanfare.

I considered this abrupt courtship as I roved the upstairs rooms the next day. Guillemette and the other upstairs girls, whose ranks I now joined, seemed pale as fish bellies compared to Maria and Cook, who tended the kitchen garden, fed the hens, and sometimes worked the fields; as such, they were the only female staff besides the farmer's wife who seemed to see the sun. The upstairs girls—hardly "girls," most of them—stalked about on stooped frames and sniffed like rabbits at the slightest provocation, or moved slowly, like figures underwater.

"Of Sire you needn't worry." Guillemette was not nearly so generous a teacher as Maria. "He has boys to empty his pot and make his bed, but you'll want to know what trunk or closet holds what, 'case he calls for something. He'll be at Morlaix all day." She looked up expectantly from her dusting. "I'm busy. Off you go and have a look around."

"And then?" I urged, afraid she would vanish again and leave me idle.

"He changes his shirt every Lord's day," she begrudged me. "He likes the robe with the wolf-skin cuffs kept on the kitchen hook under the perch for the hunting bird. He had it made special," she sniffed—as if it were *her* robe, as if they were *her* wolf-skin cuffs—"by the furrier at Valognes. And take care the velvet sword belt don't get wet. The color runs."

"But what must I *do?*"

"How should I know?" she blurted, and it occurred to me that Guillemette *didn't* know any better than I did.

The mistress has . . . limited experience running a household, a small voice had ventured at table the night before, and a fair number of the upstairs girls had bowed their heads in silent assent. As if sensing my failing confidence, Guillemette added, "She'll school you when she's ready."

I skulked about the west wing feeling desperately exposed, as if I might any moment be found out and made an example of. I wandered airy rooms with lofty oak beams, stone floors, and huge fireplaces, tested the mattress edge on huge paneled beds, marveling at tapestry canopies embroidered with beasts and foliage. I handled red, white, and green serge curtains and spotless white wool blankets as if to do so would instruct me. There were chests everywhere, deep, wide, and elaborately carved, some with heavy locks. I opened those

I could, rifling through cloaks in bloody hues, velvet hose, brocade waistcoats with ribbons, fine garments with silk buttons and shoulder knots. Once Guillemette passed bearing a fresh vase of flowers as I was lifting out a bolt of blue and white satin. "From Bruges, in Flanders," she murmured conspiratorially, and I fought the urge to knock her over the head with it.

But I had no such leisure to explore in the east wing, Milady's domain. Indeed, when she heard me humming—I thought softly—as I dusted one of the chambers at the far end of her hallway, she came and bade me follow. With thudding heart, I trailed her into a large, elegant chamber. She handed me a brush, saying my name uncertainly as if only now recalling it, and again, savoring it like a sweetmeat. *Perrette.* "I have no girl to brush my hair."

I reached out slowly, clasping cold pewter with a mermaid carved in. The brush handle was the siren's scaly tail.

When the lady loosed her black hair from the pins, it danced with static. I had to soothe and train it to the task, raking over-gently at first, afraid I'd snag or harm or otherwise offend, but she urged me on with her hand, permitting me, and to calm myself, I imagined that it was only Grand-mère's gray mane in my hands. Perhaps that siren on the brush lured me, for I slipped into a rhythm that bloomed in my throat, and it wasn't until I looked up at Milady's eyes in the mirror that I understood I had been humming aloud. It was one of

Grand-mère's old country tunes, about an elfin prince and a maiden.

Her gaze was wide and glistening. When it met mine, she looked away almost apologetically, confessing her own defeated love of music. "This we share," she said, the youthful flesh creasing round her eyes. "I knew it when I heard you out there."

Turning, she took the brush from my hand, laid it down, and held my rough servant's hands in hers. Her loneliness must have touched me even then. Blushing, I felt its chill in her creamy fingers and ached, before long, to have my hands back, to sit on them and warm them again.

I tried and failed to meet her eye as she sighed. "But alas. I have no heart for music now."

She may forget and speak to you like a sister, one girl at the table had put in, *but when she wills it, you'll sift through the dung heap. Pray, remember you are a servant.*

I waited for Milady to continue, but she only let go my hands, lifted the brush again, and began to fashion her hair into the severe style I had seen in the kitchen. I stood idly by, uncertain what to do, until Guillemette knocked lightly and said the master was returned from Morlaix. "If it please you, Mistress, he would have the household gather in the great room."

Milady went at once, her satin skirts rustling, but I lingered in the hall, anxious for Guillemette or anyone to lead the way. "Another gift, no doubt," the dour woman said with a sigh, arriving at last by my side. "Sire favors an audience."

I followed her down as others drifted in, forming a silent half-oval on the parquet. We kept our backs straight. We did not whisper. Cross-eyed Symonette, dressed in a clean smock, formally announced Sire's entrance as if the master were the lead character in a play rather than a patriarch returned from a day's business. The farmer seemed to look at me while he spoke, but it was hard to be certain. Symonette always seemed to be looking somewhere he wasn't.

Master took his time. The boy servants fought not to squirm. Milady stood looking forcibly cheerful at the center of the human horseshoe, and when he entered, taking up most of the air in the room, she bent at the knee like everyone else.

"Wife." He bowed gallantly, and she strode forward to accept his hand.

"We are grateful to have you returned to us, Sire." She kissed the hand with diligence, though her stance was weary. He revoked it with a glad sneer, reaching into his pocket. Craning forward like the others to see what he brought from his waistcoat, I realized this was an established dance they were doing, we were all doing, for could any do other than his or her part? There was no script, but no matter. Neither was there liberty or uncertainty. He gave her a gilt box. She opened it slowly, responsibly, casting long glances behind as we jostled. She let him take the box from her, helpfully, and lift out the shiny object. *Ooh*, we said, and, *Aah*. He clasped it round her neck, encircling her with powerful arms, his gaze daring her not to look away, though she did. She always did, Youen told me later, when we met by the well before supper. And always looked at the edge of tears. "He's a bully," the stable boy pronounced.

So I told him how her eyes had teared up that afternoon when she spoke of music while I brushed her hair. I found myself leaning closer as I spoke.

Youen only shook his head as if he pitied me. "Her Ladyship played the violin when she came. She wouldn't spare you or any of us a glance were she not so starved for society."

Pride rose in me like sap. Had I disappointed him somehow? Did he think me a stupid baby? I stalked off, surprising us both, I think. I glanced back from the kitchen doorway, and the Red Boy was still watching, with a hint of pleasure in his eyes.

Did Milady find her life at Kerfol lonely? Master seldom spoke harshly to her, but many days he did not speak at all. She was forbidden to accompany him on business or roam the estate grounds in his absence. "She's as good as a prisoner here," Maria confided when I paused in the kitchen with the lady's washbasin one day, her voice dropping as if the very stones in the walls might overhear. "You should hear her beg him to let her pat the chaplain's old dog."

When the baron rode off to Morlaix or Quimper or Rennes, as he so often did, he assigned so close a watch that his young wife could scarce walk from one wing of the house to the other without finding a maid at her side.

But one morning, with Master due to depart for Quimper, Milady called me in from candle making. I couldn't welcome her advances, feeling, as I often would, like a fly in her hapless web. On the other hand, we made some two hundred candles a day that season, casting them in molds with wicks or stripping the bark from rushes to dip in melted tallow for the common rushlights. It was weary work.

"Come, walk with me." She did not seem to command so much as cajole, as if I might object. As if I *could* object. She led me through the busy courtyard back to the orchard and reached to touch each branch we passed, elegant fingers trailing over knobs of bark and heavy fruit. The day was bright and blue. Her face was closed and dreamy. Against my better judgment, I found myself at ease.

But two figures back in the courtyard startled me right again. They were too far off to make out, but their stance and focused stillness told me they were likewise watching the two of us: fuzzy figures strolling in the orchard. I had a sinking feeling then, that I'd somehow trespassed; at the core of that sinking feeling was the seed of another. I resented Milady for leading me there so recklessly, for doing what I knew she would do again and again. Her need was such. I felt afraid for no reason I could name.

The first figure revealed itself. Cook came bustling across the wide courtyard, carrying in her oft-scalded hand what looked to be a shiny copper plate. By now, Milady had stiffened like a doe reading the wind. As Cook drew close, we saw that the plate bore a sliced apple, artfully composed, its flesh a perfect pinkish white.

Before the lady could inquire or accept, we saw the second figure striding forth. We stood quite still until the baron reached us, greeting Milady with a tight smile.

"I'm no queen," his wife protested with a shrug, "to need such honors." She took the plate from Cook, who looked as uneasy as I felt and who tugged me away by the apron string. We had not been dismissed, so we stood apart to give them privacy.

I heard Milady soften her complaint with a hollow, insistent laugh. "I can pick my own apples, you know, Yves. I might enjoy it."

He leaned close, lifting her chin, and his shadow darkened her. "I would have you inside now," he said. "I depart soon, and a man with a treasure does not leave the key in the lock when he goes out."

"Why do you never take me with you, then?"

So few things pleased Sire, but he seemed to smile as he fished a timepiece from his coat of dark red-flowered silk, gesturing at the house. "Young wives belong at their firesides."

Abruptly, he set off for the château again with Cook at his heels, and when he'd gone, Milady and I followed the edge of the moat around to the front gardens—so she could hear the birdsong a moment longer, she said. She hurled the already browning apple in among a stand of drooping cosmos. "When he goes, you bring me an apple, Perrette." Milady spoke over a shoulder, her voice stubborn and rueful. "That one had a worm in it."

The crunch of carriage wheels on gravel sent me scurrying down to the kitchen, where I secured a basket from Maria and walked—nay, skipped, for this was a precious errand—out to the orchard again. The day was yet crisp and fine, and just as I'd hoped and imagined, Youen found me rummaging through the gnarled branches.

"I saw you go past." He bit thoughtfully into one of the baron's perfect apples, a dozen bees circling him as if he were a honeyed treat.

"You make very free." I glanced round.

Youen leaned easily against a trunk, and his look said, *Do I?*

"Maria warned me never—"

"Maria," he sighed with good humor. "Is there nothing under the sun Maria doesn't know?" He took another bite while I stood frozen to the spot, basking in his attentions, for he seemed to study me.

Chewing and smiling, he plowed at the soil round the tree's roots with his boot heel. "I hail from a family of notorious poachers, you know. Ask anyone." Coppery bangs dropped in his eyes, and he pushed them back again. "Old Yves tried to catch my father in the act, and his father before him, for decades. Don't imagine I'd ruin my good family name by getting caught."

"But why—?"

He looked up quickly. "Why what? Why does the lord of the land hire the spawn of a known poacher?" He looked hard into my eyes, and I did not look away.

The Red Boy threw down the half-eaten apple without bothering to bury it, as I'd hoped and expected he would. "Why do birds fly?"

I watched him go, red to my ears, and then rooted out the soiled core from the thicket. I buried it in a hole like a charm.

That night I found Milady in the great hall, weeping. It was the grandest space in the manor, its ceiling painted with nymphs and animals; green and white marble walls; stately pillars framing lead and gilt statues. I stood wringing my hands as she roved the parquet floor in her rustling gown, running her hands over velvet benches and silk curtains embroidered with *fleurs de lys*. She flicked the fresh-cut flowers and painted with one finger in a sheen of dust on a sideboard, erasing her script swiftly.

I stood watching from the shadows, guilty as a thief.

"I have nothing," she said, looking up as if she'd known I was there all along. I was rapt—bewitched, it would seem. Why didn't I flee then before it was too late? Take my hemp sack and go.

She lifted and slapped down her riches, one opulent object after another, and my head reeled with confusion.

Nothing.

Like most everyone at Kerfol, I assumed it was Milady's childless state that grieved her. It must have grieved Yves de Cornault that she gave him no son, but did he fault her? Lonely though her marriage was, could she fault *him*?

But she snatched up my hand before I could ponder further. "Come, Perrette." Once more, she brought us to the orchard, now silvery in moonlight. In Milady's grip I felt the same pulsing energy that I remembered in the body of my little pet bird. Birds have hollow bones, Grand-mère had said, closing my hands round Percy's downy form. Delicate creatures. But my pet was a wild bird, and in that small, quavering shape, Grand-mère said, lived every wind that blew in every corner of the world. "Do not forget and set him down, even for an instant, or off he'll fly."

Would it be that way to hold Milady, too?

For once, and not for long, I pitied her husband.

But it took little to see that Sire was the furthest thing from Milady's thoughts. "It is a different orchard now," Anne de Cornault whispered as she skipped past and round me—mad, ecstatic, I know not which—turning and whirling under the upraised arms of the trees. "Now that *he* has walked in it."

I remembered very well, of course, the young nobleman's words at table that night, my first night in service at Kerfol.

Quiet. Quiet. You've had too much wine, I wanted to plead into the roar of crickets. On the other hand, I wanted her to speak and tell me everything. I wanted to know what would become of me, of everyone in this doomed house. I wanted fair warning if she meant to turn the master's wrath upon us all, but it was not my right. So I followed as she walked, holding her skirts like a peasant, as she wore herself out, danced her passion in the tall grass.

It wasn't until we started back toward the courtyard that I noticed she wore no shoes, that she was tramping through the damp weeds with feet as white as porcelain. I think those bare feet frightened me most of all.

That night I lay alone on my narrow pallet remembering the big featherbed. It was Mama's pride and joy when we were small—"the reason I married your father," she would joke before Papa lost his commission and the hunger came. After the hunger, there were no jokes; the featherbed was sold like everything else to stop us starving. I remembered the safety of sun-and-lavender-scented sheets and how the center of the bed sagged. I remembered my leggy sisters all in a tangle and Grand-mère perched at the edge, gruffly singing. I remembered Papa blowing out the candle, the crinkling of his tired eyes as he smiled good night.

Good night, Perrette.

I whispered it into the dark like a prayer.

Stingy of heart and nature, Master still returned with costly gifts from Morlaix or Rennes or Quimper whenever he went away. No silk, gem, or linen was too fine, and though he showered her with favors like the diamond-and-sapphire necklace, none moved her.

Until the little dog.

When Master returned early that winter from a lengthy trip to Bordeaux, he brought from behind his back a velvet box. Never had I seen him so animated, even playful. His harsh features looked almost handsome in the firelight, or at least a shade more youthful— a hint of his nature before it was steeped and thickened in arrogance. He set the box on the hearth, opened the lid, and out sprang a little golden dog.

Milady gasped with pleasure as the creature bounded

toward her. "Oh, how beautiful!" She lifted the dog, which propped his front paws on her shoulders to regard his new mistress with round, begging eyes.

After that, she never let him out of her sight, but petted and talked to him as if he were her child—and indeed, the little dog was the nearest thing she had to a child. Or would ever have.

Yves de Cornault was well pleased. A sailor had procured the animal from an East India merchantman, and the breed was much in demand at the French court at the time, so the baron had paid a steep price for it. But the dog made his wife so happy, he boasted, that he would have parted with twice the sum. He let her keep the creature with her always, even adorn it with the sapphire-and-diamond necklace—also, of course, a recent gift from her husband, one she had never much showcased till now—wound twice and tenderly round its throat.

One day as I was tidying her dressing table, Master came to her chamber door. She had fallen asleep in a chair with her bare feet resting on the little dog's back. I stood as still as I could, feigning invisibility. As if sensing him in the room, Milady woke with a start to find him there, smiling strangely.

"You look like my great-grandmother, Juliane de Cornault," he said, "who now lies in the chapel with her feet on a little dog."

This seemed to chill Milady, who pulled her shawl close round her shoulders, but she laughed. "Well, when I am dead you must put me beside her, carved in marble, with my own dog at my feet."

"Oh, we'll see." He laughed, but his black brows furrowed. "The dog is a symbol of loyalty."

"And do you doubt my right to lie with mine at my feet?"

"When in doubt, I make inquiry. I'm not a young man," he added, "and people say you lead a lonely life. But you will have your monument if you earn it."

"And I will be faithful," she replied, looking down at her hands, "if only to earn the prize of having my little dog at my feet."

He noticed me then, and I saw fury in his eyes. "Stop your staring, slut, and get about your work." He raised a hand to strike me, but I ducked and fled to the kitchen, to Maria, who fed me broth and smirked at my childish terror and trembling. "Did your papa never beat you?"

I sobbed, shaking my head, and swiped at a tear.

"Do you not see now . . . he has the right to do much worse? And exercises it. You'll learn how to walk and where to stand. Where not to stand. The best of us, the wisest, are hidden in plain sight."

"Like Youen, you mean?"

"I meant no such thing." Maria eyed me suspiciously. "But I see what's on your pea brain—"

I laughed through my tears.

"He'll mock you till the cows come home, Youen, before he'll spare you a smile."

"He's spared them." I hoped I did not sound proud. "Once or twice. But Maria, he said he comes from a family of poachers. That Sire knows it."

She shrugged.

"I don't understand. Why would the baron hire the son of a poacher? One he knew about, I mean."

Maria dabbed broth off my mouth with her sleeve. Her plump hand smelled of cloves. "What better way to keep an eye on him?"

"But Youen's father—"

"What would you have his father do? And besides, I wager the old rogue behaves himself now. Sire's rabbits are safe for once."

I hung my head.

"You see how it is?" She lifted my chin, and I found the strength to nod.

Thankfully, the master went away again. He always did.

In the baron's absence, his old aunt, the widow of a fellow nobleman, spent a night at Kerfol. She was a pious dame of great consequence, much respected by Yves de Cornault, so when the widow proposed that Anne visit Sainte-Barbe with her, how could she object? Now the lady's established favorite—a dubious honor, at best—I went along, too.

It was at Sainte-Barbe that Milady spoke with Hervé de Lanrivain for the second time, at least to my knowing. They had not more than five minutes together under the chestnuts as the rest of the procession filed out of the chapel. Before the others came out, he said, "I pity you," in a hoarse voice not without tenderness, a voice almost shy for all its bluster. Less angelic than I remembered, he was a princely creature all the same, innocent and arrogant both, lashy and beardless with dark, knowing eyes that had seen far shores yet did not once leave her face. There was no joy in a man like that, yet he was not stern like the baron. Milady, for her part, seemed surprised, perhaps that anyone outside our household knew enough to pity her.

He added, raising a hand with youthful bravado, as if to silence me or anyone else who might object, "Call for me when you need me," and Milady smiled, just slightly.

I seemed to see her smiling more often after that, usually at the window, or on those rare Sunday carriage rides while Sire was away, and I wondered in my girlish way if she longed to be with Lanrivain. I would, were I Milady, though for myself, I preferred the easy grace of Youen's nature. He was not bleak and burdened with history, not noble any more than a woodcock or a horse's muzzle was noble, but more and more he shone in my thoughts the way a spider's web shines at dawn with dew.

Here began Milady's restlessness. First she had me root out and rescue her half-forgotten violin. I found it in the attic, twisted in moth-eaten velvet, and unwound the cloth slowly, for it seemed a living thing. When I plucked a dusty string, it shrieked, then snapped, and I shuddered, drawing the fabric tight again.

Milady sent the instrument to Quimper to be cleaned and restrung, and took to playing wild, mournful melodies — when her husband was away, of course — that filled the manor with black unrest.

One night I found her so, dressed in just a sleeveless linen shift, and I winced to see a bruise, purple-yellow and garish on her shoulder. I looked away, ashamed, as if I'd found her naked, and she did not sense me and turn with those large eyes in that too-pale face. She went on playing, swaying slowly in her labor like a snake in darkest India rising from a basket.

One day while Sire was abroad and I went out to lay linen on the lavender beds to dry, I stumbled across Milady and Hervé de Lanrivain in the flower garden. He must have walked in on the avenue, for I'd seen no strange horse in the stables earlier when I delivered Youen one of the miniature tarts Maria was baking for the lady's tea. (She now let me steal away with the occasional treat. I had been warned, Maria said. Her work was done so long as I understood: at Kerfol, no crime was too small.)

Drawing back among the shrubs, I heard the young noble say that he would depart in the morning for a foreign land. His mission was not without peril and might detain him for months. When he begged for a remembrance, she glanced down shyly and sidled off after her little dog, returning with something held close to her chest. Though she concealed it from unseen eyes like mine, the necklace glinted in the sun like a blade. As he leaned forth to accept it, their two foreheads met, for just an instant, and the glare of gems was muffled.

When Master came home days later, he absently scooped up Milady's pet from her feet to pat it. His broad hand hovered a moment, almost imperceptibly, over the place where the precious collar had become a fixture. Though he did not speak, his aspect changed, and the animal squirmed and whimpered to be let down.

Setting aside her embroidery, Milady reached out, but her husband withheld the poor creature. No one who hadn't fearfully studied Sire's manner would note a rebuff, but I did. Milady did.

"I'm afraid he lost it in the undergrowth of the park." She did her desperate best to charm, to seem at ease, craning all the while toward the little dog in his arms. "Ask Perrette. We searched high and low."

I must have winced to hear my name. Or did I nod calmly and carry on stitching like the other women in our fireside circle? Milady had indeed enlisted half the manor to search for an object she herself had "lost," though I did not, would not, say that she had. Not to anyone. Certainly not to the baron. What's more, her monstrous lie had bought us the better part of that morning in the sunshine while our chores languished. Youen's hand had brushed mine as we hunted side by side in the rosemary, and the touch made me shudder and smile all day, constantly. Stupidly.

Sire had no mind for my or any view. He released the dog and watched intently as it trotted away.

His mood at dinner was bland. He talked at length, describing what he had seen and done at Rennes, pausing often to search his wife's face with cold eyes. He went upstairs early and would not be accompanied or disturbed.

The mood below suffered.

Milady snapped at Cook and nagged Maria pointlessly over household matters she knew nothing about. When our mistress saw that she had strained their patience, she set off pacing the great hall at the front of the house. She ordered all the candles lit, though it was late and there were no guests to entertain. Once the candles blazed, she thought better of it and had them all snuffed out again. She opened doors and closed them again, but thankfully did not flee to the gardens or the forbidden orchard. She stared out at the black night. She stole looks at the stars. She mourned what was to come.

When at last she called for me to dress down her bed, we took the stairs slowly, carefully, like elderly women afraid of slipping or breaking a bone. We did not hurry, but we arrived all the same.

We found it.

The little dog lay dead on her pillow.

She did not scream, my mistress, or complain in the slightest. You might think she had expected it. But all the grace and power I knew her to possess in that slight frame seeped away then. Her shoulders stooped. She crept forth, confused, and we stood united in horror. The animal had been killed with the sapphire-and-diamond choker, the one Sire had given her in front of the entire household, the one I knew she had furtively given to Lanrivain in the hedge garden. The necklace was twisted thrice round the dog's slender throat.

Milady scooped up the rigid, small form and unraveled the gems, which seemed to burn her fingers. She flung the necklace against the wall and thrust the little dog at me, as if I should know what to do. Waving us away, she lay lightly across the bed. Her shoulders—bruised, I knew, tender under fine fabric—moved with silent sobs.

With Youen, I buried the dog by candlelight behind the chapel. We did not speak. He would not look at me.

Horror had silenced us, and when I tried to tell him what I knew about the necklace, he hissed me quiet. He stepped hard on the dirt over the small grave to tamp it. He made a quick cross with his heel. He left me alone as the sky began to drizzle.

I followed him back. "And where is *justice?*" My naïve words echoed horribly through the stalls, the candlelight making our shadows garish. A gelding down the row answered with an indignant snort. Youen caught my wrist. "There is nothing just in this world, Perrette. In this house—and what more of the world belongs to me? To us?"

Lightly but with his whole body, he steered and pinned me against the inside of the mare's stall, silencing my lips with his roving fingers, rubbing a scratchy cheek against my cheek as a bear rubs its back against a tree. I clutched the candle for dear life though the holder dropped in the hay. My cap slid down, and our breathing made a rhythm, and though I wished and feared he would, he did not kiss me.

The stamping mare recalled us, and he stood me back with eyes like a forest burning. He turned my shoulders, steering me round heaped manure toward the stable door, and whispered softly into the nape of my neck, "Good night, Perrette."

Youen sent me forward as a child releases a butterfly, and I slept without dreaming.

When the baron went away, Milady hovered by windows or paced and made a sublime screeching with her violin. Had she heard from Hervé de Lanrivain? we wondered. Kerfol buzzed with gossip day and night. Would Master let his young rival live, knowing what he must know? Had he already killed Lanrivain? Or just deprived him of the necklace? The same necklace that had killed the dog. I'd scanned the floor and peeked under the bed the next morning but found no murderous glow or telltale shimmer. "Who would confront him if he had?" I wondered aloud.

Day after day, as Milady sat stitching by the hearth with us, night after night alone in bed, she must have wondered these things, too, and anguished, and against my instincts, I ached for her. Questions lapped at my lips like a tide some days, and to hold them back brought a kind of nausea.

As I stood brushing her hair one night, I noticed that she had not worn her silken robe over her shift to conceal the bruise. I touched it with my forefinger, tentatively, and she caught my hand — and then she kissed the hand, almost gratefully, and I fought the urge to draw it back.

"I am not very much older than you are, Perrette."

I nodded in the mirror, feeling suddenly wise and very old indeed. I looked a stranger in the glass, while Milady looked familiar. I seemed to know her now.

"I used to think there was no fate worse than not being loved," she told me — told herself — in the looking glass. "But now I know there are worse things."

When Master was home evenings and smiled across the table at her, I saw that she would not solicit news of her friend or send a trusted servant with a letter. Sire was sure to find out if she did. I imagined — I'm sure we all did — that he could find out anything.

That winter was black and long and rainy.

Youen grew increasingly drawn and distant, taking his meals alone in the stables. He didn't speak when I brought them, only grunted thanks and stalked away into the mare's stall. He would sit among the dung and flies rather than with us. Rather than speak. And what could we do? What could I do? Some selfish, disbelieving part of me drew away from Youen in turn, because I did not fathom, could not fathom, what he might need, what might heal him, and failing shamed me.

What girlish innocence I still had thrilled when minstrels arrived at Kerfol with a troop of performing dogs. Overjoyed and forgetful, as lovers are forgetful, and with Sire away, Milady bought the smallest and cleverest, a white, feathery dog with one blue eye and one brown, and sat with it on her lap through supper, feeding it scraps.

But when her husband returned from his travels, she came from her bath one night and found that dog, too, strangled on her pillow.

On yet another evening, Youen found a poor, lean greyhound whining at the gate in the bitter cold. Against his advice, Milady took possession of the dog and hid him in a room that no one went to, surprising us all by smuggling food there from her own plate. But Yves de Cornault was not long recalled from business when we found the greyhound stiff and strangled, a tiny wisp of blood on the pillow by its mouth.

Another time, when his wife had merely stooped to

pat the chaplain's watchdog, a grave old pointer who slept in an anteroom of the little church, the baron happened up the path unexpectedly, and by nightfall, the pointer, too, was gone from Kerfol.

"Who next?" our ranks whispered. "What now?"

When Youen graced us with his sullen presence at all, usually only at Sunday's meal, he refused to comment on the dogs. He would get up and leave the room if pressed. He was never one for gossip, Maria said, but he also had more feeling for animals than most. Once Sire nearly beat to death a young horse he was breaking, and Youen had lunged for the whip. The master struck him hard that time with a ringed knuckle, and the cut on Youen's brow had shone an angry cinnamon for days.

Milady mourned her losses bitterly, vowing to me never to bring another dog into the manor, no matter what. But longing lasts, while memory is short. Yves de Cornault was on business in Rennes that endless winter when a brindled pup was found in the snowy wood out behind the chapel, its leg mangled in a trap. She warmed and fed it, wrapped its leg, and hid the animal in the west wing until the blacksmith came on an errand. Milady paid handsomely for his confidence, and the good man agreed to bring the dog back to the village and care for it.

But that night we heard whining and scratching at the door, and when Milady opened it the lame puppy jumped at her with frantic little barks, drenched and shivering. We hid him in her bed till morning—when Master's carriage wheels sounded on the gravel.

She closed the dog in a wardrobe, closed me in the room with the dog, and drew a finger to her lips as she backed out and shut the door. I listened to the coachman leading the horses out back. I strained to hear the soft bustle of servants gathering downstairs to receive him, and Milady's voice—too high for a moment, until it found its liar's pitch.

The puppy in the wardrobe began to bark.

Frozen, I pleaded in my thoughts for it to stop, and for just a moment, as if Fate would tease me with her wit, it did. But all sound below, too, had ceased. The house held its breath. I cracked the wardrobe door and the dog snuffled and nudged under my hand. I heard footfalls on the steps and eased the door shut again, but it was Youen who came. "Where is it?"

I pointed.

He went and like a magician put his hands on the dog, silencing it with his strokes. He leaned over to shield and muffle it, and at length crawled in and pulled the pup between his raised knees, still stroking and soothing. "Perrette," he hissed, for I was still frozen. "Shut the wardrobe door."

"But—"

"The door. When he's at table with his wine, tap once at the chamber door, and I'll smuggle this down and out through the buttery."

"He'll—"

"He'll not hear me." He nodded helpfully. "Shut it."

I did tap, and Master did not hear Youen sneak the creature down and out to the stables. Or so we thought.

But when I went with Milady to turn down the bed, we found the animal like the others, dead on her pillow. She moaned and blinked, incredulous, while I, not awaiting her order, wrapped it in the blanket. I ran with my burden banging against my back down the stairs and out through the twisted trees in the orchard, where I left the bundle under the stars for the crows before racing back to the stables.

Youen did not move when I tried to rouse him from the straw. He could not. His ribs were broken. I knelt and turned his face to me, and one side was bruised like the darkened side of the moon. His inner ear was caked with blood. I stroked his fine, fiery hair, and he groaned, so I ran for Cook, who could nurse Youen and ply him with herbs.

After the puppy, all was quiet for many weeks. Master acted ordinary enough. The days passed slowly— and the nights, bleak and horrible now that I knew Youen less and less and longed for him more and more. His injuries were healing, but his silence was impenetrable.

We none of us spoke of Lanrivain without crossing ourselves, but one night a peddler woman came to sell trinkets to the maids. Milady had no heart for trinkets but stood looking on as her women made their choices. At length the peddler convinced her—I heard not how—to buy a peculiar powder box for herself. When all was quiet once more, Milady took my hand and closed us together in the library, where she sat turning the odd, pear-shaped container in her hands.

At last, she opened it and fished a rolled strip of paper from the powder. "Turn away." She hid the paper from my eyes. I knew who must have sent it, though I saw no seal. As Milady read, my own hands began to shake, for I could well imagine the penalty for complicity.

She dropped Hervé de Lanrivain's sentiments into the fire, and I saw the spidery script on the page cringe and fold in upon itself in flame. When she waved me out, I was glad to go.

Youen was not in the stables. I sat shivering behind the woodpile until I saw him return. I found him in the stall of his favorite horse and knelt before him. He looked up with difficulty, as if his head were too heavy to lift, and I searched his eyes. I held his jaw in my hands as the mare stamped and tickled the top of my head with her flicking tail, but Youen brushed my arms away stiffly, his eyes blank.

"He sent a letter," I urged in a whisper. Surely this would rouse him. "Lanrivain."

Youen winced. He rocked forward, knocking me

off balance, and his torso curled over his raised knees. I righted myself and stroked the top of his head. "Please, Youen. What can be done?"

"It's not from him."

"What isn't?"

"The letter." He lifted his head, his eyes familiar again, flashing.

"You must tell me."

At long last he blurted in a voice like a child's, "I mustn't tell." He shook his head, his eyes glistening. "I mustn't tell."

"Youen—"

He lurched to his feet, and I followed him out of the stables, along the edge of the courtyard. I ducked after him into the winter orchard. He was stealthy and quick. We ran over the icy, cracking earth, well beyond the orchard where I had never been before, until my side cramped and my hem and stockings were full of burrs. Ending in an owl-haunted meadow, we stood under a round moon, panting.

"There." He pointed.

I looked down and saw nothing. Frosty grass and gray, flattened milkweed.

"He's there. Lanrivain."

I stepped back, the horror dawning on me. "You can't know that," I soothed, for he was broken now. My Red Boy had fallen to his knees by the grave, collapsed forward in the cold, and his back was heaving.

I bent and stroked it gently as I could, though I was afraid—so afraid—of this place, his pain, the world. "How do you know?"

He rose up, spent, then knelt again, staring into the bare trees like a wild animal. His eyes no longer glistened. His voice was flat and strange. "Because I buried him."

He stood, brushing himself off, and spoke over his shoulder as he went. "Sire bade me do it, and you may tell what gossip you will, but it will be my life."

It was the last time I saw him.

The baron retired that night after dinner. Milady sent me up with a cup of hot wine, and Sire waved me out again with word that he was not to be disturbed.

Later, in her room, she took my hand, looked hard into my eyes, and swore me to secrecy. Lanrivain would come to the courtyard that night to wait for her, after the moon had set.

I gaped back at her, mute as a fish.

"Listen at his door," Milady pleaded.

Lanrivain was dead. Did she not believe it, too? After all, the necklace had found its way back, but many weeks later, the young noble had not. My eyes swam with tears as I remembered Youen at the dog's grave, his boots black with earth, digging intently. Quietly. His red hair dark with the sweat of his labor. *Poor love,* I thought, for what help had I ever given him? What help had I given anyone but myself?

"Go and listen," Milady urged. "Please."

Steeling myself, I crept past the second staircase into the master's wing. Down the hall. I leaned by the keyhole, hearing the vigorous breath of sleep within, rasping, regular. I was shaking so much when I came back that Milady had to stroke and soothe and endure while I ranted under my breath of werewolves.

"Superstitious girl," she complained to calm herself, I think, for she must have wondered if her husband was really asleep. Or was he only acting at sleep? "You're a peasant, but the priests are no better."

She wouldn't let me turn down the bed but bade me lie down beside her, though we didn't sleep. We stared at the ceiling. I longed to speak, to caution her, to save us both the error I knew she must make.

I wished many things. That I had been able to read the letter before it curled in flame, the blue-burning script, for I felt half mad with not knowing. Papa had been the only one on our farm who could read, and when the rare letter stained with salt arrived, we huddled in candlelight while Papa read of cousin Étienne's travels in the New World. The Indians he met as a trapper there had a name for every moon, my cousin wrote. Harvest moons and milk moons. A beaver moon. And the hunger moon of late winter.

This was the moon Hervé de Lanrivain chose to light his way back to us.

✦ ✦ ✦

When first I came to Kerfol, it was still Grand-mère's *loup-garou* I imagined out circling the manor walls in moonlight. He might lope beneath my window or leap up on the gable and look in at me through silvery lead panes. Such scenes distracted from an empty belly.

But when the *loup-garou* became Youen, I wondered, would the animals in his stable whimper and stir and bump one another in fear at his coming, or would they know and trust and forgive him as I would surely know and forgive? As the moon moves the tide, it pulls and shapes the werewolf's bones like dough, and so I enjoyed imagining Youen's pale boy-form being shaped and reshaped, made and unmade, and these tender new terrors worked on *me* like the merest tide, making the nights hot and exceedingly long. I might wake and contemplate creeping into the buttery for a stolen berry tart from Cook's cabinet, imagine ripping at the flaky crust, scooping and mashing the sweetness into my mouth, sucking blood-red fingers, for I was starving. Starving.

Every moon at Kerfol was a hunger moon.

The moment I met him, Youen became my *loup-garou*, and this was a girl's fancy, feverish and exciting but never horrible. Grand-mère's version, on the other hand, was a beast that stalked in shadow, ripping the dogs to ribbons.

Youen was not our monster.

It was Master, two-faced and terribly transformed. He was the inside-out beast that hunted in the night. He had killed Lanrivain—and perhaps penned the note himself, staged this drama to entrap his wife, to confirm his suspicions about her—and the wretched procession of dogs, and he would kill us all.

About this last, I was also wrong.

That night, not a year after the little golden dog was brought to Kerfol, Yves de Cornault was found dead by the narrow flight of stairs leading down from his wife's rooms.

It was Milady who found him and cried out, poor wretch—for his blood was all over her—and at first the roused household could not make out what she was saying. We came running, afraid for her sanity, but there at the head of the stairs, sure enough, lay the baron, stone dead, the blood from his wounds dripping down the steps. He had been scratched and gashed on the face and throat, as if with a dull weapon, and one of his legs had a deep tear in it, which had cut an artery and probably caused his death. But how did he get there? Who had murdered him?

Hearing his cry, Milady was roused from sleep. She rushed out, she said, to find him slumped.

But *could* she have heard? the prosecution argued. The walls were thick. Her room was at the far end of a long hallway. She was fully dressed when the others arrived, and her bed had not been slept in. What's more, the door at the foot of the stairs was ajar, and the chaplain noticed that her dress was stained with blood around the knees, that there were small bloody handprints low on the staircase walls.

Might not the blood marks on her dress have been caused when she rushed out of her bedroom to kneel by her husband? Or was she downstairs when her husband fell? Had she felt her way up to him in the dark on hands and knees, stained by his blood dripping down on her? Though the open door below and the direction of the finger marks on the staircase seemed to support the latter view, Milady held to her statement for two days.

But on the third day, word came that Hervé de Lanrivain, a young nobleman of the neighborhood, was wanted for complicity in the crime, though none had succeeded in locating him. Two or three vaguely disreputable witnesses came forward to confirm the local rumor that Lanrivain was, at one time, on good terms with the Lady of Cornault, though people no longer associated the two of them in light of his extended absence from Brittany. Many, myself included, knew that he was dead, buried in a wild meadow out beyond the orchard—murdered by the baron—though this evidence was not, of course, admissible. Not if we valued our lives. And yet . . . I had seen the rolled message. I had even thought I glimpsed, when Milady's scream woke me and I ran to the window, a hatless, beardless figure pacing below in the courtyard, a white glimmer of loose shirt.

But we at Kerfol had long since ceased believing in what we saw.

One witness was an old herb-gatherer suspected of witchcraft, another a drunk from a neighboring parish, and the third a half-wit shepherd. "He was pale," the half-wit kept saying furtively, wringing his hands as if this point were of secret import. "Very pale."

"Speak up," barked the judge.

"He was white as winter," said the half-wit more confidently, like a dog with a prize bone.

The prosecution would require more definite proof of Lanrivain's involvement than the herb-gatherer's claim that he had seen the young nobleman near the wall of the park on the night of the murder.

It's not clear what pressures were put on Milady, but on the third day, when she was led into court, she seemed weak and vague, and after being told to collect herself and speak the truth under oath, she confessed that she had in fact gone down the stairs to speak with Hervé de Lanrivain but was surprised, before she could reach him, by her husband's cry and fall.

I was the first to answer Milady's scream by the stair that night. Her eyes were too hollow to read, her hands too bloodied to grasp in comfort. If only I had not succumbed to sleep, I might have stopped her. Stopped *this*. I shuddered on the cold step, looking down at him. *Or died trying.*

Her one thought as we lay side by side in the stillness, waiting for the moon to set, must have been to get down the winding staircase without stumbling, unbolt the door, wave Lanrivain to safety, and steal back to her room.

We had tried the bolt earlier in the evening, even applying a little goose grease from Cook's storage. But it would squeak anyway. Not loudly, she told those assembled in the courtroom, but the sound had stopped her breath. And sure enough, not a moment later, she heard a noise above.

"What noise?" the prosecution interrupted.

"My husband . . . calling out my name and cursing me."

"What did you hear after that?"

"A terrible scream and a fall."

"Where was Hervé de Lanrivain at this time?"

"I believe he was standing out in the courtyard. I'd made out a form in the darkness — and I hissed, 'For God's sake, go,' before pushing the door closed again."

"What did you do next?"

"I stood at the foot of the stairs and listened."

"What did you hear?"

"I heard dogs snarling."

"Dogs. What dogs?"

I shuddered at these words, and Milady bent her head, speaking so low that she was told to repeat her answer: "I don't know."

"What do you mean — you don't know?"

"I don't know what dogs."

The prosecutor rubbed his hands with satisfaction. Those who had been long in the household, including Maria, now testified that in the months before his death, Sire had suffered the same dreadful fits of silence as before he was wed, though none reported signs of open disagreement between husband and wife. There had been none.

None that would impress these men.

And what cause had Anne de Cornault for going down at night to open the door to Hervé de Lanrivain?

Her answer caused a stir in the courtroom. She went because she was lonely, she said, and wanted to talk to the young man, though she had not managed it.

Was this all?

"Yes," she swore, "by the Cross over Your Lordships' heads."

But why at such an hour?

"Because I could see him no other way. He had sent a note."

A smug exchange of glances across the ermine collars under the crucifix.

"I burned it in the fire," she added quickly.

"What did you want to say to Hervé de Lanrivain?" the prosecution asked.

She answered: "I wanted to ask him to take me away."

More murmuring. "Then you confess that you fled to him with adulterous thoughts?"

"No."

"Then why did you want him to take you away?"

"Because I was afraid for my life."

"Of whom were you afraid?"

"Of my husband."

"Why were you afraid of your husband?"

"Because he had strangled my dogs."

Another round of bemused murmuring circled the courtroom. Noblemen had the right to hang their peasants—and most exercised it—so pinching a pet animal's windpipe was nothing to make a fuss about.

Her statement was curious, the judges agreed, but what did it prove? That Yves de Cornault disliked dogs? That his wife—to suit herself—ignored this truth? And did she imagine a little spat justified her relations, whatever their nature, with her alleged accomplice? Absurd! Even her own lawyer tried to interrupt her story, but she went on as if hypnotized, as if reliving the scenes of her narrative in her head.

The one judge who had shown a certain tolerance now demanded, "Then you would have us believe that you murdered your husband because he would not let you keep a pet?"

"I did not murder my husband."

"Who did, then? Hervé de Lanrivain?"

She shook her head sadly, fiercely. "No!"

"Who, then? Speak."

At that point, she collapsed and had to be carried out of the courtroom.

✦ ✦ ✦

The next day, the prosecution ordered Milady to continue her deposition, opening with: "Tell us exactly what happened. How long did you stand at the foot of the stairs?"

"Only a few minutes."

"And what went on meanwhile overhead?"

"The dogs were snarling and yelping. My husband cried out. He groaned once, I think, and was quiet."

"And then?"

"I heard the noise a pack makes when it's thrown a piece of meat."

There was a collective groan of disgust in the courtroom. "And all this while . . . you did not go up?" the judge asked.

"Yes—I started up—to drive them away."

"The dogs?"

"Yes."

"Well?"

"When I reached the top of the stairs, it was dark. I groped and lit a candle, and found him lying there. He was dead."

"And the dogs?"

How Milady trembled. I longed to go to her, shield her from those gawping men, hold her slender shoulders still, but I had neither courage nor will, any more than Maria or Cook or the two dozen others who bore witness to our sorrows had. Youen, whom I had not seen since the night of the murder, was not present. I only later found out why.

The crowd in the courtroom held its collective breath. "The dogs were gone."

"Gone. Where?"

"I don't know." She straightened herself to her full height. "There was no way out." She shook her head madly, as if her hair were full of bats. "And there were no dogs at Kerfol. There. Were. No. Dogs."

In the instant before I and Maria and the judge came forward to calm her, there was a confused uproar. Someone on the bench cried out, "This case wants a priest," and the courtroom erupted in squabbling.

Witnesses confirmed that there had been no dogs at Kerfol for months. The master of the house hated dogs. No question.

Long and bitter discussion ensued as to the nature of the dead man's wounds. An attending surgeon spoke of bite marks. Witchcraft was suggested, and at length Anne de Cornault was brought back into court at the insistence of the judge.

Where could the dogs have come from?

She did not know.

He persisted, almost gently. "Do you think that you could have recognized these dogs — had you heard them before — by their barking?"

"Yes."

"And did you . . . recognize them?"

She swallowed, whispering, "Yes."

"What dogs were they?"

"They were my dead dogs."

Milady was escorted out of the murmuring courtroom, not to reappear. There was a church investigation, but in the end the judges disagreed with each other and with the church committee. Anne de Cornault was released into the care of her husband's family, who shut her up in the tower of Kerfol. There she died, many years later, a harmless madwoman, and I watched it happen.

We grew old together.

Every love she or I have ever had within or beyond the borders of Kerfol has been wrenched from us, until honest love began to seem a peril in its own right.

On the eve of the baron's death, I later learned, Youen had left Kerfol a blathering idiot. It took a fortnight of my ruthless badgering for Maria to confess this, for she knew what the Red Boy had meant to me.

Perhaps he had confronted the baron. Perhaps he had been caught trying to run away. In any case, she had only glimpsed him after the last beating, his ears a bloody pulp, boxed so often they oozed. She had seen the pauper's wagon come for him, had watched his poacher-father, a big man with hands like hams, weep as Cook wrapped the wool blanket round him like a shroud.

I tried to summon the courage to seek them out, send a message to Youen's village, but rumor came that his family had moved away.

A year after the trial, Maria, too, vanished, fleeing

in the night with the blacksmith's son and a rag full of silver spoons. Glassy-eyed Cook read me the note in halting fashion, and after, we never spoke of Maria again:

> My dear Perrette:
> Do as I do.
> M.

The spoons were returned to the cabinet one day not long after, without comment; I know not by whom: one or another of the baron's heirs. When I found the first of those familiar spoons in the drawer, I held it up and found my own distorted reflection in the shine, dull eyes that could not weep.

Milady and I spoke not of these matters. We spoke almost never, though our sorrows united us. I kept close by her, especially when the moon swelled and paw prints dotted the mud round the moat come morning. But when our wrists brushed as I washed or dressed her, we flinched as if stung. To touch, to know affection, was to suffer, and we would not bring that upon ourselves, upon each other. For what judge, what God, would hear us?

I will labor till my last days in obscurity, scrubbing cobbles in the gray light of morning, and—like paw prints in rainfall, like Milady in her madness—fade and be forgotten.

Only this house, only Kerfol, which I once imagined so neglectful, will remember.

These Heads Would Speak

1802

*V*ICTOR WOULD BRAVE THE WALK from the cross-roads, he said. He needed air.

In truth, he didn't want to go on with them to Quimper.

Mother struggled out of the carriage to kiss him with all due (on this day) ceremony. Thanks to him, she would have her old life back. Not all of it, surely, not Father, but there would be ease and security again, some degree of luxury: what degree this staunch new democratic world would allow. *Greedy woman,* Victor mused, watching her tame her big bustle of skirts. *Is it not enough that we live?*

He didn't want to go with them and listen to Michel's maddening whistling the whole way, but he didn't want to lose his way through the heather or sink into a bog, either, or catch cold or meet strangers or otherwise face the unknown without Mother. "Won't you at least call at Kerfol," he urged, "and take your rest first?"

For a moment she ignored his question, going on at length about the caretaker. "His name's Grenier. Jean Grenier, and his daughter is Marguerite. See that our rooms are ready and have them plan dinner for sundown. Oh, don't look so, Victor," she cooed, tweaking his chin. "My darling." She kissed her fingers and pressed them to his cheek, leaning close. "I never rest. You know that."

Michel, their one remaining servant, stopped his infernal whistling long enough to extend a hand to help Mother back up, and she stuck her coiffed head out the coach window, waving strenuously as they started on their way again.

Victor watched the coach grow small on the horizon.

He stood like a statue on the cart road. A signpost at the crossroads promised a dozen paths, and for a moment he imagined losing himself on one of them. But like that of the rest of his accursed class, Victor's way had been laid centuries before he was born.

He obeyed the arrow reading KERFOL.

Mother would meet with the lawyers today on behalf of his fortune. Not his yet. But it would be, if she had her way—next month, when he came of age. A widowed great-aunt had left all of her still-vast estate to a nephew she scarcely knew because she was childless and because he was a child left fatherless by the revolution. She also knew that Victor aspired to be an artist, meaning that he would be penniless and without prospects. "Thank the Lord for her romantic nature," Mother had gushed when the letter came, and Victor saw with disgust that she would have kissed every corn on the savior aunt's feet had the crone still been standing.

Victor came in at an avenue. The trees had the tall curve of elms and the ashy sheen of wet olive trunks and formed a long arch that soft April light couldn't penetrate. *If ever an avenue led unmistakably to something,* Victor thought, *it was this one.* It seemed purposeful, while he was not.

They'd rented Kerfol to be on hand for the legal proceedings. Arriving without the heir in question to huddle with the lawyers and the faction of the family now controlling the estate might present certain challenges, but having Victor there would do more harm than good, Mother had said. His murmured replies and offensive daydreaming would undo her efforts.

Victor wanted no part in any of it.

Snidely—*legitimate business will not involve you, but maybe architecture will*—or just helpfully, Michel had recommended the tombs in Kerfol's chapel, which were rumored to be magnificent. The only servant they'd held on to through the Terror, the only one who hadn't fled, taking a healthy share of silver and brocade with him, Michel held a special status. He might be a capable, badly disadvantaged relation—knowing Victor as he did—and they both resented it.

Michel was right about Kerfol, though. It must have been the most romantic house in the province once. Victor would have been happy to remain on the stone bench at the end of that long avenue, absorbing the influence of the place. He looked up at the sky, an uncomplicated blue, and almost hoped that Jean Grenier wouldn't turn up. Not yet. He rifled through his leather satchel for pen and ink, found a rumpled sketchbook, and began to compose the entryway and the chiseled hedge garden beyond, coiling mysteriously into shadow.

But soon the distant, silent house with its grim towers — and the many empty avenues converging where he sat — began to unnerve him.

He knew nothing of the estate's history except what Michel had told him, but it had to be impressive. The accumulated weight of countless lives and deaths always lends majesty to an old house, but Kerfol seemed to harbor more: stern memories, cruel memories stretching away like its gray avenues into a blur of darkness. *Tombs in the chapel?* he reflected, aware of the sound of his own breathing. *This whole place is a tomb.*

All of France, it seemed at times to Victor, was a tomb, full of hateful echoes.

Still, he wished the caretaker would not come. Hearing the facts about the house would chip away at its overall impressiveness. *I'm told it's the very place for someone of your sensibility,* Mother had said. Meaning what? Excitable? Oversensitive? Inclined to embellish? What would she tell them in Quimper? He was nearly of age, after all. Wasn't that what these proceedings were all about?

Besides which, it seemed impossible that Kerfol could be "the very place" for *any* living soul. Sensing that he would learn less by looking than by *feeling* what the place had to communicate, Victor followed the moat around back. In stark contrast to the methodically shorn hedges out front, the rear of the château was a riot of weeds. Apart from a wide patio checkered with red, white, and black marble tile and edged with urns and the chapel, all the rest — the old courtyard, the dovecote, the orchard — had been more or less reclaimed by the wild. Even the stables and servants' quarters, still in use, were carpeted round with moss and cloaked in vines.

An arched iron gate hung open in invitation, so Victor ducked through into a dense tunnel of wisteria. Hanging flowers diffused the sunlight and made him feel like he was walking through a storm cloud.

At the other side was the path to the chapel. Victor didn't take it. The tombs were there, he knew, just over the rise, but instead of a tourist's curiosity he felt again the heaviness of Kerfol's unknown history. He began to look for signs of the caretaker.

As he was heading back through the wisteria tunnel, a little dog appeared and barred his way. It was a handsome golden creature with round brown eyes, but Victor didn't like dogs. They'd lurked round the prison, rooting in dung heaps. They'd been there in Paris, he now recalled, before his father got them out during the September Massacres. Mobs armed with sabers, clubs, and knives had hijacked priests from their carriages in those dark days, hacking them to bits in the streets while the National Guard idled. The same rabble had roved from prison to prison, holding court. A "judge" interrogated prisoners, sentencing them to death no matter their testimony, parading their heads on spikes. Exhausted executioners napped among heaped body parts, it was said, and when a woman brought bread, it was soaked in the blood of the dead before it was eaten. Passersby would note red running under the prison walls, out into the gutters, and the dogs of Paris noted it, too.

To quiet his heartbeat, Victor moved forward to try to pet the trespasser, but the dog retreated. Feeling a trespasser himself now, he returned to the patio. The animal had vanished, most likely in the overgrowth pressing in at the edges of the patio.

He circled the estate and rang the front bell, relieved by the expanse of trimmed hedges all round. He'd once heard a courtier claim that the rigid geometry of French royal gardens was a mark of triumph over nature, of civilization over barbarism; to seize and snip unruly twigs, to bend back wanton blades of grass, was to assert dominion. *Better see to things out back, then,* he mused, smiling at his own jumpiness.

All he wanted now was to find a window with good light and grind some pigment for paint, let the fitful colors crowd the darkness from his mind. Weariness had settled in every inch of him.

A wheezing man saw him in. Jean Grenier was brusque and fat and spoke quickly, without meeting Victor's eye. "I've had the girl dress down the first two rooms in the east wing. Up there." He pointed to one of two staircases. "I trust your mother . . . Madame will favor the view of the hedge garden. I'll set your things in the room across the hall." With a grunt, he took Victor's bag and vanished, just as the dog behind the château had vanished.

Victor wandered out of the great hall into a narrow passage leading to the rear of the house and the kitchens. As quickly as her father had gone, young Marguerite appeared. His first glimpse of her was in a flour-coated apron, for she was baking, whistling a jaunty tune. She was curvy and capable. Apart from Michel, Mother hadn't kept servants for years, and their finances kept them out of society. As such, Victor had lately had little contact with any female but his parent. He stood quietly in the doorway, appreciative and suspect.

"I grant you permission to stare, sir."

He went right on doing so, stunned.

Marguerite shrugged and her dark brows peaked, as if to say, *Well, why shouldn't I speak so to my betters?* "I'm not your servant, after all. I'm not employed by this house. You *will* need my permission."

"Perhaps you should accept it as my compliment," he warned, rehearsing for the day when he *would* again command a houseful of servants. If Mother and the lawyers had their way, it would not be long. They'd lived simply after Father's murder at the hands of rev-olutionaries — Marat's devils and Robespierre's — but he was his mother's son, and he'd do well to claim his place. "Your father is in my employ," he managed. "In a manner of speaking. Is he not?"

That seemed to chasten her, so he smiled to show he thought no less of her for it.

"Yes," Marguerite complained, "and it's but for the grace of God I don't leave him to fend for himself."

Victor leaned with his elbows on her tall work-table, enrapt by her strong arms kneading, her deft hands smoothing the flour. Mother never let him near the kitchen while she worked. It mortified her to be seen with her sleeves pushed up, even before her own son. Work, housewifery, these were shameful tasks — though what aristocrat hadn't likewise suffered?

Unlike Mother, Victor was not *re*claiming anything. He remembered very little of the Terror. His memories were a wash of color running in a gutter. He remem-bered a Festival of the Republic, held in a church, and a gaunt man in a red cap booming from atop a tall chair: "Long live the nation! Long live the republic! Down with priests!" while revolutionaries rushed the altar and side chapels, smashing statues, paintings, ornaments, reli-quary shrines. He remembered his mother offering the warden chiffon for his wife's hem and liver-spotted hands unwrapping Father's linen, slicing up his bread, breaking the pastries they brought him to eat. He remembered mobs gathered outside the prison walls, chanting, "Give us the enemies of the state! Give us the traitors to the nation!" and that his father's eyes seemed to sink deeper into his skull with every visit. He remembered that one day, Father just wasn't there. "Removed to Paris for trial," barked the woman with spotted hands. Mother had covered her own mouth as if she might be sick.

He found himself drawn into Marguerite's orbit that day. Her easy spirit pleased him as much as her shape, though her confidence was no girl's. It was a woman's, and unsettling. Was she that much older? Who knew with peasants, whose hands were rough and who aged before their day? Watching her work, he could only admire the strong, soft flesh of her arms, the creamy skin showing over the stained bodice. She had a smudge of flour on one silky collarbone, and he fought the urge to erase it with his fingers.

"Was that your little dog outside earlier?" he asked to break the silence.

At first she looked confused, and then a veil of intrigue dropped over her face. "There are no dogs at Kerfol."

Before he could argue otherwise, Marguerite burned her plump arm on a wall of the hearth's bread oven. She shrieked, fanning the air as smoke flew out from between the bricks, and his question was forgotten.

He was rudely awakened the next morning by the dream of the empty executioner's basket. Again his father's head rolled merrily down the scaffold steps, the fish-like mouth forming words he could not hear, the eyes a hollow blackness. Victor hadn't been present, thank the Lord, when Father was beheaded, but in a way he wished he had been. After, the only way to endure the image of his father's toppling head was to construct a hero who'd never been. Someone who'd struggled against savagery and injustice. Someone who'd died trying.

Everything around Victor supported this lie.

Mother seized on Jacques Ange Bertin's character-ization of Father in his letter as a man who "died on his honor . . . conducting himself with such dignity and accord that even the executioner winced to see the blade fall." What left her lips after that became family his-tory, but for Victor, her tale of savage glory only served to make a stranger out of the man he most loved. Father became a faceless hero, a bloodied ghoul that plagued Victor in dreams—especially once he'd read German anatomist S. T. Sömmering's letter in the *Paris Moniteur.* Victor vividly remembered the date: November 9, 1795. *The guillotine is a terrible torture! We must return to hang-ing!* This was some four years after the national razor had replaced the noose as the official executioner's tool. *Do you know that it is not at all certain when a head is severed from the body by the guillotine that the feelings, personality, and ego are instantaneously abolished . . . ?*

It took years to bring back the mild and smiling man Victor remembered, to restore in mind—and to mourn—the whole and loving and largely unimpressive man who'd been his father.

Bad dreams woke him, even still, like the thump of a blade.

It would have been an uneasy sleep anyway, waking in a strange bed, sunlight barred by heavy velvet drapes that had only recently had the dust beaten from them. They reeked of it. Everything in this damp, old château stank of some other time. But he had an eastern room, and the light was good.

Before she left for the day, Mother had sent Michel with breakfast and his easel and gear. There was nothing to do but rise and shine, as she would say in that relentless, cheerful way of hers. *Rise and shine,* he told the sun bitterly.

The first sketch came with the clarity and suddenness of a dream. A faded portrait in red crayon. Her face was small and oval-shaped. She had a thin mouth and a delicate nose. Her eyebrows were as lightly penciled as the eyebrows in a Chinese painting, her forehead high and serious. The arrangement of the black hair, fine and thick in appearance, was demure, and the eyes were shy and steady at once. A pair of beautiful long hands was crossed below the lady's breast. She was a lady, no question. Not a lively wench like Marguerite, but a true—if imagined—lady, and he felt pride and an odd shame at having presumed to create her. Victor had lost his wealth and his father under a single sharp blade and with them, Mother said, his confidence.

"Marguerite," he called the next afternoon, for she was just outside his chamber dusting in the hall. "Does she look familiar?"

She came and studied the sketch, gnawing a savaged thumbnail. "No." She shook her head. "Should she?"

He felt disappointed somehow, as if she might have read something in the fine features as an astronomer reads the alignment of planets.

"What do you need with her?" Marguerite demanded, contemplating his work with grudging respect. "Am I not pretty enough to draw?"

A compliment, he guessed, for who cared to be drawn by a lesser artist? Did it matter that he'd impressed a girl like Marguerite with his talents? No, but he was used to being indulged and humiliated by his mother and tutors, who only barely concealed their disdain for his mediocrity. This was something else, something more — even Marguerite saw that — and in a way it scared him.

Victor looked at his hand, at the crayon, and back at the paper. Who was she? Who was he to have created her? Could he trust that it would happen again?

It did, though it was not the *same* woman. She was altogether different, his second subject. For days Victor worked furiously to prepare a wooden panel.

He slathered it with gesso, sanding and layering and sanding again. All that week as Mother schemed with lawyers, he ground pigments, cadmium and cobalt and ochre, mixing them with linseed and walnut oils. He sanded and sketched and in due course began to paint, moving from broad brush and palette knife to the little miniver or squirrel-fur brush for the fine details of the eyes.

Those sea-green eyes, her pert lips, seemed to him already present on the panel somewhere, existing beneath gluey gesso layers sanded soft as eggshell. He had only to tease her forward from below. He even tried to explain this to Marguerite, who was surprisingly sympathetic for her class. "I hear it is like that," she said with hands on hips, leaning in. "For artists."

Was he that, now? An artist? Or was Marguerite just too ignorant to withhold the term, as others had done—his tutors, Mother, even Michel, who made an amateur's survey of art and architecture?

There might be a little of Marguerite in this painting, after all, in spirit if not aspect, for Jean Grenier's daughter got him painfully worked up at least twice a day, though he lacked the ambition to seduce her.

Unlike the lady in the crayon drawing, the painted girl was a clear translation of fantasy. This long-necked blonde was his match, Victor imagined, sweet and arrogant with a knack for withholding. A careless, slightly dangerous girl with a pout. He painted her in a traditional gown, simple and nondescript, but while the glaze dried, he imagined her bare in the big stone bath at his family's ancestral château, surrounded by the cerulean blue of Moorish tiles and the white flicker of candles.

To immortalize his daydream, he painted her in a splendid necklace of sapphire and diamonds, gems as watery as the shimmer of bathwater in candlelight. She deserved whatever delight he might offer, for the sadness in her eyes — less defined than that of the woman in the sketch but more subtle in the end, more masterful — made him want to protect her. *You have the look of someone damned,* he thought. *Someone who doesn't know it yet.*

Again, Marguerite's interest surprised him. "Her neckline's a bit severe," she offered from behind. "And that white's overdone."

He did not look up from his palette knife but wiped his brow with the palm not covered in paint. "Spoken like a true Paris art critic."

"It's too milky, that neck. Too tender." She laid her hands on his shoulders, and he stiffened. "It begs the blade."

Was she speaking madness, or was he too inclined to perceive it? Had he misheard? What did Victor really know about the peasant breathing down his neck, or she about him?

He laughed it off — what choice had he? — and let his shoulders relax under her warm hands. And yet he wondered, were Marguerite and her father *that* brand of peasant? Like the *sans-culottes* who tore Princess de Lamballe limb from limb during the September Massacres, parading her head—the bloody hair cleansed and primly curled—on a stake beneath Marie Antoinette's window? Why had it taken Father so long to spirit them out of there? he wondered, letting his mind wander from Marguerite, who went on watching him work. When it had been worse than degrading to stay?

"They have shut us in," Mother had complained to her husband as Victor hid behind a tapestry, kneading the cat's velvet ear in small fingers. He did not know who "they" were or how his family could be considered shut in when they came and went freely, albeit only on foot and in strange, simple clothing.

"When will you *do* something?" his mother had pleaded, and this was a terrible thing, for Mother never pleaded. "Will you let them cut our throats at their convenience?"

At long last their family, like many others, had fled Paris with but a fraction of their furniture, servants, and horses. They got by peacefully for a time in Brittany, where Mother's family had also decamped, but to show the slightest trace of rank in those days was dangerous: even a spoon with a coat of arms on it might land a man in jail, and before long, Father did land there, no matter their crude efforts to blend in. Perhaps they had delayed in Paris too long, arriving too late and too obviously. They would never know what forked tongue had exposed them. Police in the provinces, anyone prepared to enlist a tribunal, were rewarded for ferreting out aristocrats, priests, and other counterrevolutionary suspects.

Would Marguerite and Jean hiss and gossip at the tavern tomorrow when they went for their annual two-day outing?

"You were going to tell me," he demanded, his voice harder than before—no longer playful—"why you and your father go to town every year on that day." Victor set down his paintbrush but lifted it again for the security of holding something. "Tomorrow."

She averted her eyes. "You should come with us. I know you're too good to be seen with the spawn of Jean Grenier, but you'll wish you had."

"Why? There are amusements in town?"

"You'll laugh if I say. Call me a superstitious peasant."

"You've never seemed troubled by what I thought before."

"Trust me."

"Give me cause—"

"I won't let you make me a fool, but call it an anniversary. One it's our custom to avoid. Papa and I are never here on that day."

"*What* day, Marguerite? You're being very coy." He felt himself warm to her again. It was his great failing, this willingness to be led.

She heaved the water bucket to her other hip, and Victor enjoyed the view of her body in motion. "You're too proud, yes?" she said. "To trust a woman? And who is this ice princess? Your paramour?"

He breathed Marguerite, ripe and sweet, but in the dark of daydream he imagined himself in a candlelit bath with the languid girl in this painting, her shadowed eyes staring back at him. "Tomorrow may be my last day at Kerfol, after all. Mother threatens to have her precious papers by nightfall. Stay with me, Marguerite." He reached for the arm balancing her bucket, a teasing lunge, but her nimble hip eluded him. "Stay, and let your father go alone. Play with me."

He tried to meet her eye, but she only scoffed and tipped a slow stream of well water into his lap. He looked on with only mild astonishment, wincing.

"There's what I think of the fire of your loins, schoolboy."

Marguerite parked the bucket back on the bone of her agile hip and brushed past. "You're in my path," she said. "Go and paint your little pictures in the garden."

Wrenched from dreams faintly recalled, of tender throats and throbbing veins, he woke determined to hitch a ride to town on the hay with Jean and Marguerite. But when he lurched half-dressed out to the stables, their cart was already gone. The dark of the stalls yawned back at him.

He would relax into a day's work. He could do that, forget that Mother would return greedily endowed with his future, with one fate or another that was not his choosing. He had faced worse.

The light was buttery and kind, though he knew he would want shade later. Victor carried a portable table out to the rear patio, arranged paint pots and brushes, went away, and returned again with the easel. He sat regarding his nearly finished painting, breathing the good stink of turpentine. He worked, and took pleasure in the work.

But it seemed to matter, too much, that he had missed Marguerite and her father. He felt vaguely panicked, surveying the vast sweep of foliage threatening to swallow every surface beyond the patio but the chapel, which hunkered now in shadow.

He lifted a dry brush, idly plying its bristles, and when he looked up again, there was the golden dog again, not ten feet away on the marble tile.

In a funny way it was as if time had looped backward, as if this were somehow, again, his first day at Kerfol, his first sighting of this animal. Had the days between—the waiting for Mother . . . the cheerful, empty exchanges with Marguerite . . . the reckless success with crayon and brush—been a dream?

He'll bark in a minute, Victor thought, *and someone will come.* But no one would, he knew. Not today.

Call it an anniversary. One it's our custom to avoid.

When the forbidding little animal kept its distance, Victor decided to act before fear disabled him as it had disabled his father in Paris. He would chase away the foolish dog and proceed indoors to the library. Kerfol was exactly the sort of house that someone, at some point, felt compelled to write a history about. That history was no doubt in the estate library, easily accessible. He advanced bravely, but as the dog drew back at his approach, another one, a rough brindled thing, limped forward.

There are no dogs at Kerfol. Had Marguerite not said as much?

But now a third—a long-haired white mongrel—slipped in from the edge of Victor's vision to join the others. All three stared at him with grave, shining eyes, but none made a sound. They fell back on muffled paws, watchful as he stepped forward.

Charge me, then, he thought stupidly. *Isn't that what packs do?*

They let him retreat beyond the patio as he pleased, following at a distance, always the same distance, always with Victor in view. He paced nervously, aimlessly at the edge of the barrier of overgrown thickets, trying not to trip over ornamental urns, grasping his useless paintbrush.

He breathed deeply, striding in under the canopy of dangling wisteria, and crossing to the chapel path. He still hadn't managed to visit the fabled tombs of Kerfol, so he sauntered up the rise, thinking to do so now, impressed with his own bravado. His own maturity. What a fine and civilized diversion! Art. History. Architecture. Father had always indulged these pursuits (though never Mother, unless he begged; she would have him shut in with numbers all day). Some of Victor's favorite memories involved childhood trips with his father to museums and menageries and the private cabinets of great men. Once, as they stood before an enormous nautilus shell mounted to form the body of a silver-gilt swan in one of the Medici collections, Father lay a hand on Victor's shoulder.

"I'm not the ineffectual brute she makes me out to be." Perhaps he thought Victor too young to grasp or retain such a statement, to equate "she" with Mother. "I like quiet," he concluded. "That is all. There is far too much fuss and bother in the world for my liking. When at the end of the day"— he'd paused to stroke his only son's boyish mop of hair—"the sun still sets."

Victor stopped now in his tracks.

In the dark glass of one of the long gothic windows of the chapel, the head and torso of another dog appeared, a white pointer with one brown ear. This was a solemn old soul, larger and more assured than the others, staring out, intent. *How did you get in there?* Victor wondered.

Victor hurried back through the tunnel, only to find the rest of the pack waiting on the patio. There was a newcomer with them, a shivering black greyhound with pale eyes, that hung back from the others.

Victor stood a full five minutes in that grim half-circle, waiting, as the dogs appeared to be waiting. They wouldn't bar his approach—Victor knew that somehow—and he thought they must be abused, to cower so silently, though they didn't look hungry or maltreated. Perhaps they were no more damaged than he, the jumpy son of a murdered man who'd never felt on his own behalf an instant's physical pain or real discomfort. Only Victor's mind had suffered, Mother said. His nerves. And what sort of man did that make him?

At last he steeled himself and moved toward the golden leader, stooping to pat him with a nervous laugh. The little dog did not start, or growl, or look away. He simply slipped back a yard or so, paused, and held his watch.

"Well—*what?*"

As if their movements were tied to his, the dogs separated when Victor stalked forth. "Go ahead, then," he barked. "Growl. *Do* something." They glided forward again, and he backed off through a thicket, making somewhat pointlessly for the stables. Twigs slapped his face and sprang back with a dry rattle, and he was so consumed with relief when he could no longer see them—apart from the old pointer, who went on staring plaintively from the chapel window as if waiting to be let out—that Victor nearly collided with an old brick well concealed in the undergrowth.

He rubbed his hip, tried the crooked stable door, and thought better of it, seeing the futility of his goal. He also saw a clear path, a full cart road, really, leading down from the stable door along the side of the property. He took this merciful route now, laughing at his idiocy, almost enjoying his stroll, the cheer of birdsong. When the road split off, with one side leading down to the front gate and the outer avenue and the other hooking back along the hedge garden toward the château entrance, he hesitated a moment, but only a moment, before making for the house.

He wanted nothing more than to return to and huddle in his bed. *She'll come home soon,* he thought irrationally, *and see my things outside.* He longed for Marguerite's teasing laugh, and it occurred to him that he not only lacked a father; he had never had a sister or brother to tease or be teased by. As before, the safety of the open sky, the bright, butterfly-laced hedges, lifted his spirits.

He made for the broad steps.

And there they were again, the dogs, the golden one a little ahead of the others. The black greyhound shivered beside a triangular shrub. They were everywhere, it seemed—one here, one there—stationed behind tidy hedges, fanned out in a design of their own accord as if to mock the unknown gardener's studied pattern. *They form their own maze,* he thought wildly, *and to enter it is to die a madman.*

"Stupid animals!" His voice startled even him. The dogs stood motionless, ears alert. Perhaps they had lived too long with people who never spoke to them, he thought now, grasping for sympathy. Their coats were smooth, and none but the greyhound seemed too thin, but their strange passivity seemed even sadder than the misery of starved and beaten animals. If Victor were a man like Michel, he might draw them into a game or a scamper, but the longer he met their fixed and weary stares, the more preposterous that idea seemed. The dogs knew better, it seemed. They knew what this place would and wouldn't tolerate.

In the end, it was as if they held in common one memory so deep and dark that nothing since had seemed worth a growl or a wag, rather like Victor's own notions of his father under the blade of the guillotine. How could he wish to be a man after that knowledge? Did death not dwarf all expectations? All ambition?

What these dogs most suggested to him was loneliness beyond reckoning, and he tried to imagine his father's loneliness under the blade. Had they thrust a hemp bag over his head? Could he see the sky through the fabric? Were there bits of blue, Victor wondered, to soothe his eyes, and did white clouds reel past, perhaps a seagull circling — or some better, brighter bird? Was it all blinding brightness in that last moment? All color, like the world when Victor closed his eyes or let his vision blur, let the brush lead him . . .

Maybe Mother and his succession of tutors were right, and he would always be a child, painting unexceptional pictures. *Except one,* he thought with grim pleasure, remembering the girl on the easel across the courtyard.

When he arrived at the patio, the dogs had already stationed themselves on either side of his worktable like sentries. He laughed out loud at the absurdity of it. The dogs shifted uneasily. What were they waiting for? What could he give them?

When will you do something?

Though the portrait was on the other side of the easel, he held her face in mind with desperate clarity, and at almost the same moment that the dogs began to stir, he remembered Marguerite's words. *That neck begs the blade.*

Real or imagined, the words struck him with fresh horror, and he blundered to the easel with closed eyes, shooing back the dogs, and now Sömmering's words swarmed into his thoughts like wasps. *Furthermore, credible witnesses have assured me that they have seen the teeth grind after the head has been separated from the trunk.*

Victor opened his eyes long enough to snatch the painting up under an arm and gather the paint tray to him like a child from a burning bed, and then he closed them again, with surprising determination. *And I am convinced that if the air could still circulate through the organs of the voice . . . these heads would speak.*

He felt paint ooze over his wrist as he strode past the wretched watchers into the gilt-and-mirrored shadows of Kerfol. Once inside, he dared to open his eyes, hurried to a bench in the great hall, and set her down beside him. He held the board in two trembling hands as he might the shoulders of a lover.

Yesterday's glaze had dried, and his soul's mate

seemed to watch him, craning her tender neck, and he knew then that they were but two dolls, poppets, playthings. Whom would he love in a world of play? Playing house, playing lovers, playing at a future?

Do *something.*

He took up a paint pot, the first he snatched, red cadmium—a good, dark color—and began to slap paint straight from the pot onto her face. He heaped it onto his palms, the oily slap a pleasure against his skin, a joy in his nostrils. With hands slippery as a surgeon's, he swiped and fumbled for the big boar's-hair brush. He slashed at her pretty eyes, erasing what could only suffer, saving her.

Before long, much of the panel was a blank red stain, and his heart beat hard as he strode to the big front door and opened it again, his hand leaving a bloody smear on the doorknob. The dogs were there, dotting the lawn, perfectly still. Soundless as before.

He eased the door shut, though they would not pursue him. Again, he knew this. Somehow. Still he staggered to the stairs, tripped, and fell forward on his hands. Victor walked up on all fours like prey, leaving a pattern of handprints.

Mother woke him in his bed, but only after the trunks were packed.

In a silky bustling of widow's silk, she peeled the covers back and cursed the paint everywhere. "Oh,

Victor, not *you* as well as the stairs!" She barked for Michel, whose footfalls came nearer. "Victor, look at you. Covered . . ."

He cringed like a child as she heaved the blankets away, curling out of her reach. "I don't care if I never come back here," he told the pillow, feeling the full wrath of his father's memory.

"Look at you . . . foolish boy. You're not well again. Up, now!" She slapped his behind, and he rolled sullenly away. "See what Mother has for you in the carriage . . ."

"Or if I die penniless —"

"You'll have that chance after I'm dead. Only then, my boy —"

The servant heaved him up with that drab, knowing expression Victor hated. Michel, who had lifted him before, seemed especially despicable now, with his strong forearms hooking Victor's armpits.

"Take me from here," he begged. "Those dogs —"

"We'll take you . . . if you'll stand *up*."

He did, and Mother held his sticky hands high for Michel to rub with turpentine. "What dogs, Victor?" She held him clear of her silks — not wishing to squander her newfound wealth so quickly — as Michel shoved and groped him with the rancid rag. "Hadn't you better learn to control these fits? You're an heir now." She smiled at Michel, and together they led Victor blithering down the staircase, out into the empty yard, over the pebbled drive, into the waiting carriage. "A man of means."

He breathed the good smell of horses as Michel snapped the whip and Mother snatched a page from the coach seat, rattling it gleefully in his face. "The ink is dry, my boy. Rejoice."

He cast one last look down the avenue, growing smaller behind them, and knew he was forgetting something. Something he would not recover, and even as Mother stroked his pale forehead, it was already a dim memory.

"My own little man."

The Figure Under the Sheet

1926

*T*HIS PARTY WAS A BORE, like so many parties, like so much of life after Stan—an ocean away from Stan. Heels stomping out the Charleston. The moat outside full of floating vomit and cigarette butts. Sinks full of shaved ice and French champagne, and a bathtub full of gin. They were in France, sure, but Prohibition was a hard habit to break. Half the fun of doing *anything* was knowing that you weren't supposed to, and cathedrals and pretty gardens aside, you could take these wealthy sheiks and shebas off to Europe, but you weren't going to get them far from the bathtub, really, and when they got there, they'd be pie-eyed and pissing on the lawn.

Speaking of sheiks, the most momentous thing that had happened all day was the arrival of Emily's telegram from Connecticut. Valentino was dead, and half the country—"the better half," wrote earnest Emily in her telegram (it was comments like that that sometimes made Suze wonder if her prude of a cousin even *liked* boys)—was in mourning. More than one love-struck farm girl had actually hanged herself from the rafters of daddy's barn. Over a movie actor. But what an actor. What a face. Sitting in the dark, no matter with whom, to watch Rudolph on the screen was to feel every fiber of your body awake and screaming for something, anything, and quick.

Suze sat smoking in the garden among the bees, her hand shaking—nerves, coffee, too few meals—the music a distant buzz at the back of the big stone mansion. . . . The band was getting drunk. They were off-key. Young couples strolled along, enjoying the sun on their faces, and Suze did the same, steady on her feet for once because the last line of Emily's telegram ("I heard Stan's sailed off to the Caribbean again") had knocked her sober. Anyway, Daddy was due back from business in Rennes tomorrow, and she had a lot of cleaning up to do—a lot of supervising from her garden chair, anyway.

She thought of Stan on his little yacht under the Caribbean sun. The same sun now shining on her. She felt its warmth on her cheeks and bare shoulders, on her belly, still flat beneath summer linen, and she imagined Stan at sea, a nursery rhyme playing lazily through her thoughts:

> The Owl and the Pussy-Cat went to sea
> In a beautiful pea-green boat.

Like his father, Stan was a boatbuilder by trade, a craftsman who could carve and sand and stain wood to make it glow. Like gold, people said. Even her father said so. "An alchemist," he'd joked once, "like me." Daddy was a stockbroker, and making gold out of base metal was exactly what he and his kind did daily.

Despite his disapproval—nay, forbiddance—of her relationship with Stan, Daddy liked him. Suze knew he did. But Stan was what her father called "a bad risk." He was spontaneous at best and reckless the rest of the time, a gambler like his own father—losing sporadic if significant sums, which he earned catering to wealthy clients in New York and New England.

"Maybe he just needs guidance, Daddy. Don't you remember what that was like? You had help. You have to remember what it felt like . . . to have talent but need help."

"I remember, and I see what it's cost me."

"But you *don't* see."

"*Here's* what I see, Susanna. Every time your grandfather looks at you, he's not sure if it's your mother looking back at him from those pretty doe eyes, or me. We need to make sure it's her. Otherwise you'll end up coming in the back door. Like I do."

"You do not."

"In spirit. I do."

"Stan loves me."

"He loves your money."

"I don't have any money." She smiled gratefully. "You do."

He ran a light hand over his perfectly parted and oiled salt-and-pepper hair and straightened his bow tie, English driving cap in hand. "It's your mother's money, and she's dead, so we may as well admit it's your grandfather's." He was straining, she could tell, already on the move, though her pleadings held him here. For now. "I've learned how to invest it. That's my contribution."

"That's plenty."

"But I lack manners, says Gram, and yours leave a lot to be desired. I don't want them to write you off as they have me. I don't want you to disappoint them."

"Like I've disappointed you?"

"You've had everything."

"On a silver platter. And you came up from nothing and resent me in advance for blowing it all to bits. Because that's what I'll do, Daddy, if you don't let me have what I want, if you don't let me have Stan. I want to go home to Stan. There's nothing else you can give me anymore. I'm drowning in *things*." She swallowed. "There's nothing else I want."

He grinned that guileless grin of his — ill timed, Suze thought, as she was battling back fresh tears, but it usually had a gift attached, so she decided to give him the benefit of the doubt.

"Not even this?"

"This," she saw, looking up through her lashes, sniffling, was a beautiful antique sapphire pendant set in an elaborate choker of waved white gold, inset with diamonds. The whole effect was worthy of Poseidon.

She reached out, but he pulled it back, his grin wavering. "Now, this one's not for keeps. It's far too much for someone your age, but I know you like to play, and this holiday's yours, so enjoy. It's something from the estate safe. They let me use it, evidently forgetting they had a few things gathering dust in there. Shame to see it go to waste. But take care. I mean that, Suze. That's a pretty penny there, and I have a few pennies, but I'll bet that thing has a history if it's languished this long."

Suze pouted.

"I'll make it OK. I always do—make it OK. Don't I?"

She hung her head, thrilled and humiliated by her own willingness, her vast good fortune. But she let him clasp it behind her neck, though it took dedication and prying of the chin to get her to look up and seal the compact with a smile. Yes, one more season would bring her to her senses. One more spin round the globe. One more shiny gemstone. "Thank you, Daddy."

"My pleasure." He kissed her forehead. "I mean that. It brings me pleasure, you know, to make you smile. To see you happy. With everything I've got, it's all I want."

Then why do you work so much?

Suze fingered the jewels and let herself feel ashamed: not to admit a little shame made her an ingrate. There were things to be ashamed of, things she could only begin to contemplate this far from Stan, all this way round the world in a musty old castle in France.

At least she'd had the sense to hold the party outdoors, apart from the stream of spilled gin and watery boot prints up and down the stairs and out to the back patio.

Though she couldn't see his face from this distance, she watched the gardener, a sturdy Breton in a straw hat, move deftly among the geometric maze of shrubs like the ones they'd toured at Versailles, only smaller, and then down to the briars along the edge of the old wall bordering the wood and avenue. She had seen him before, and he seemed to radiate easy purpose and competence. He was older than Daddy, say late fifties, with youthful, squinting eyes in a leathery face like the fishermen in postcards she'd bought while they were touring Lorient—when Daddy, intent on helping her forget Stan, had even spared a few days away from his accounts.

Those eyes were experienced in a way the same-faced people indoors were not—of earth and the wild sea and babies. She absently caressed her belly, thinking that his sun-lined brown hands would have dirt under the nails. They would be as at ease gutting a goat or seasoning a bouillabaisse or bouncing a *grand-bébé* on his knee as they were coaxing things to grow. Emily would accuse her of romanticizing the poor out of guilt. But it was one of the things Suze loved about Stan; despite his breeding, people were people to him, plain and simple. *Real.* He made friends wherever he went, with busboys and sailors, cigarette girls and nurses, and she knew Stan would like this old gardener, too.

One drunken night of late, she'd even had a funny urge to sneak up behind the old guy, turn him her way, and kiss him square on the lips just to see those crinkly, kind eyes light up. She liked him. A man like that had something to teach her, she imagined, unlike Daddy, who kept the better part of his wisdom to himself.

She primped her bob and crossed the moat, then sashayed down the vast hedge garden toward the exit and the radiating avenues, where he had disappeared, assuming it was him. She hadn't had a good look at him this go, after all, but the straw hat was a giveaway.

The music grew dim and distant the farther she got from the house, and she had the unreal feeling she often had at parties, that she was an invisible specter passing among the living. She half-believed she could pass through them sometimes — the girls with their bare heads still wet from the ride in on a running board, frenetic, dancing in beads and flapping galoshes. The boys with oiled hair and baggy pants and *love me* looks.

Sometimes she wandered through a whole party without speaking to a soul, apart from squeezing someone's

elbow in greeting or feeling a light ginny kiss on the
back of her neck, some furtive flirt wanting to take
Stan's place. But who would take Stan's place? Who
could? Especially now. *Now,* she thought, over and over,
an incantation. But that was as far as she got. Thinking
was overrated. Without Emily on hand to scold her,
she would just rest in how unreal it all seemed. Ever.
Always. *Now.*

> *O let us be married! Too long have we tarried:*
> *But what shall we do for a ring?*

She would lose herself among shadowy laughers and
dancers and lovers leaning close to whisper and tease,
blowing smoke into the air like the stranded at sea send-
ing up rescue flares. Bumped by the frenzied dancers, her
world went fuzzy, and ironically, she drank to bring the
edges back. Drinking did that, briefly—she had once
tried to explain this to Emily (of all people)—and
then things went all fuzzy again, worse than before. But
for a moment, in between, there was clarity. This was
that moment.

As the earth leveled out and the gardener came into
view, she half imagined he might save her. She could
befriend him as Stan might do, and he would advise
her. At the least, like some fortune-teller, he could look
once into her eyes and read her shallow future. "Beware
of water," he might say, "or strangers with dark eyes."
She heard the under-music of the bees, saw the covert

swooping of a bird here, there, and felt the innocence of bright sun, and was as glad as she'd been in months.

"Sir," she called when she knew she was in hearing distance, but he kept moving along the hedges, serenely clipping, as if listening to music of his own, a slower, richer sound. She called out again, and this time he turned, almost reluctantly, and set down the clippers. He rose slowly, as if it pained him, and then clasped his hands behind his back like a priest, but she saw at once that she'd been wrong. It was not the gardener.

He was roughly the same height, squat but sturdy with fearsome eyes and a fierce-boned face framed by a pointy gray beard. His skin was coarse and pallid. He brought his hands back, wringing them once in a restless gesture that undermined his air of patience. His nails were not blunt and dirty, but long and perfectly filed on large powerful hands with dark hair that made them glow almost paler. The simple gardening tool looked strange in his grasp, like a sparrow in the mane of a lion.

"Mademoiselle?" He did not smile, and Suze felt suddenly ashamed, as if she had done something wrong, something dirty. (She did wrong things on principle, whenever she got the chance, though she kept it clean, also on principle. Would Stan have her back otherwise?)

"I thought you were the gardener." She glanced curiously at the clippers in his powerful hand.

He nodded, his eyes not exactly downcast. Noncommittal.

"Do you work for him?" she blurted, looking away from that hawk's stare. "The moat needs tending. It's full of slop."

He nodded pleasantly enough, but it was clear that he either did not understand her French—it had never come naturally to her, as Mother would have liked, and she knew no Breton—or that he was holding something back, his mouth clenched in the effort not to sneer. "The moat," he mimicked absently, in a thick accent. And then he grinned, looking her up and down: from the butterscotch silk dress and seamed stockings she had so coveted in Chicago last year, wanting them so much, so desperately—why did she want things so much and have so little in the end?—to the borrowed necklace, and it was a cruel grin, candid in a way that unnerved her.

"Thoughtless, pretty thing," he said, and the words sounded garbled in his throat. "If you were my . . . daughter," he added furtively, and she craned toward the missing words, that tide of unreality washing over her. His eyes no longer appeared watery but a dark and brutal blue, like black ice. "I'd beat you senseless."

Suze turned on her heel, stumbled, ran without looking up the sloping lawn, across the polluted moat that yesterday had been a placid black ribbon sprinkled with moss-green pollen.

"Where, love?" crooned Gerard, who was loitering in the great hall when she burst in and announced an intruder. Gerard was the ill-mannered English friend of a cousin of a friend of somebody's French relation. Who knew what was going to show up at a private party anymore? Was there such a thing as a private party anymore? A private moment? She pointed toward the front avenue. "Out there." Weary and shaken, Suze could not remember the last time she'd been alone and content to be, except while dressing in the mirror, and even then the glass seemed to tease and deceive or shine with disappointment.

No longer shaky inside, she wondered, had Gerard and friends hired that man in the garden to frighten her for their own amusement? She imagined them in an unheated upstairs bathroom somewhere in the vast château, powdering and painting dark circles round his horrible eyes. Nice Halloween prank, were it Halloween. Or was the old man yet another indolent stranger, some village hanger-on here for free gin and good champagne?

No. Gerard So-and-So had not read her thoughts or engineered anything, she realized; he was just contemplating the stains on her dress. "Who's the lucky jazzbo who got to roll in the green grass with *that*?"

That?

"Why are you in here?" She struck an imperious pose. "Didn't I ask Peg to keep the party outdoors? Daddy doesn't—"

"Daddy," Gerard purred, "does what Suze tells Daddy to do. No worries there."

"Shut up."

He blinked as if stung. "But that's discourteous, Susanna." For a moment his affront, subtle and blistering, was so convincing that she didn't know what to think. Suze was about to reach out and pat his shoulder in apology—ever the mindful hostess at barely eighteen years old—when Gerard puffed out his cheeks and sprayed her with warm champagne, laughing as he preceded her down the unlit hallway.

When she strayed into the library after him, she found a petting party in progress, with the few who weren't going at it in shadows gathered round a lanky, good-looking boy whose name she couldn't recall. He was stretched out on silk pillows on the floor, reading to them from an old book.

"There's a man in the garden," she announced, and only one or two in the crowd looked up, bleary-eyed and smiling politely.

"What sort of man?" asked the lanky boy, eyeing her strangely. His accent let on that he was a local. Was the man in the garden related to him somehow? Were they plotting something?

"Not old exactly, but in any case, he doesn't belong here. He said things—"

"What sort of things?" asked Peg, Suze's old standby, a rich acquaintance whose parents had been only too happy to send her away in Suze's untender care. Peg had an arm draped over the lanky boy and clearly wanted to hear the rest of the story he was reading.

"Things. I don't want him here. I want him out of here."

"Where's your driver?" one of the men asked. "Where's Saul? He'll make quick work of him."

"He's gone to town for more ice." Suze was aware that her voice had climbed to high and whiny and that she was losing her audience to the lanky boy, who had flipped ahead a page and was peering wide-eyed at the page to generate suspense.

"I'll show you," Suze insisted. "Come with me."

"She just wants us back outside," murmured someone.

Grumbling ensued.

But Gerard, more curious perhaps than concerned, helped herd them up and out. They all trekked, stumbled, or sashayed down the grassy hill on the west side of the mansion with Suze at the lead — feeling vindicated, safe, restored to her throne once more. The girls took off their heels and swung them with abandon and began to moan about Valentino and bicker about which film was best.

"*Four Horsemen,* hands down!"

"No, no, *Blood and Sand.* That tight little matador number was to die for —"

"You'd think he was some kind of Chicago gangster or something," Gerard complained, "with a funeral like that. I read that a hundred thousand people filed past his coffin. "

The incline led down toward tall hedges and the

shadowy avenue of trees that seemed to go on for miles at the estate entrance, and there was no one in sight, and no sound but the distant music from the band playing at the back of the house and the low hum of bees.

"We were just saying, Suze, you remind us of the princess in this old Breton folktale Tres was reading." Peg looked at the lanky boy, ill dressed for this crowd if handsome in a brooding sort of way.

Suze took his free arm, the one Peg wasn't affixed to, as Peg cooed, "That is your name, isn't it? Tres?" then burst out laughing for no reason. Nerves. Everyone had flowed round the crisply carved hedges and through a gap in the border wall. They ducked under a terrace of wisteria into the mottled shadows of the avenue. It was lifeless and eerie under those regimental trees, with some half dozen other avenues radiating out. Even had someone been lurking there, they would be long gone now and could have taken any number of routes out. Or in.

Gerard smiled coyly. "Well, it looks as if your ghost has gone to bed, Dahut."

Suze looked at him with all the scorn she had in her, without a blessed clue who Dahut was, fed up—for he'd been a rude bore since he came, aggressive too, which meant he wanted to sleep with her and knew full well in advance she'd turn him down—but before she could speak, the lanky boy, Tres, pulled the book out of his coat and flipped it open to the dog-eared page.

Suze knew better than to scold him for abusing estate property when she herself was wearing a perhaps-priceless necklace borrowed from the safe in the master bedroom. Come to think of it, Tres seemed to take more than a passing interest in that necklace, glancing at it whenever he looked up, rarely meeting her eyes afterward, though when he did, it was with a brooding directness that pleased her.

"To recap," he said, clearing his throat. "According to legend, the lost city of Ker-Ys was ruled by the good King Gradlon. The city was protected from the sea by a dike, and its gates could only be unlocked by a silver key in the keeping of the king.

"Gradlon had a spoiled daughter, Dahut, born to him of the beautiful fairy queen Malgven. He loved her well and provided for her even better, but Dahut grew up to be a young woman of, shall we say, loose morals."

Someone snorted champagne through his nose, and a wave of snickering washed through the eleven or so assembled.

"She spent her time at balls, imbibing wine and mead, and leading the local youth astray." Tres smiled, and suddenly Suze was sure that he had never been invited at all. He very likely was, as she'd suspected earlier, someone from town, who'd heard about their rental and the parties. The servants were different in every outpost. Some of those they borrowed or hired on from the owners were docile and willing, others begrudging and in need of discipline. Daddy rarely thought about the help or the movable household, except to provide for it, and urged her to speak up as necessary. But some buried part of her did not wish even a servant to think ill of her. No matter how entitled she was, she would never be entitled enough, evidently; a trait from her father's side, she guessed, though his hardscrabble roots let him thumb his nose in the end.

The servants in such places always wagged their tongues, and it seemed as if every lowlife with something to buy or sell or mooch eventually found his way to her parties.

"One day a handsome prince arrived at the royal palace," Tres continued. "Dahut fell hard and promised him whatever he desired." The impostor met her eye for the first time, and when he whispered, it was as if the noisy group around them faded out and he were speaking only to her, and then she saw, behind the lanky storyteller, a shadow rounding the bed with clippers. Clipping the hedges, moving slowly.

"That's him!" she cried. "There he is." And the party seemed to flow back to life, limbs unlocking, voices resuming. Suze dragged Tres with one hand and Gerard with the other and assaulted the man, demanding to his back that he identify himself at once or she would fetch the authorities.

But when he turned, it was only the old smiling Breton gardener, the real McCoy this time, nodding his cap politely, his sun-crinkled eyes bemused but patient with youthful indiscretion.

Suze laughed, letting go her protectors' hands. She buckled, she was laughing so hard, her heartbeat plummeting, and maybe it was nerves, but to save face, she strode forward and followed her earlier whim. She kissed the good-natured old fellow quickly on the lips, which left him stunned and possibly mortified, the butt of some wealthy brat's joke. She felt she had betrayed rather than pleased him somehow. The gardener wiped his mouth primly, turned, and disappeared into the dappled avenue with his clippers.

Suze spun round to face her wayward party — drunk with hilarity and savoring her mistake — and waved them back toward the house.

"That's some fiend you've got there, Suze," said Gerard as they climbed the lawn. "What's more, if that's how you treat an intruder, I hope to have the pleasure of trespassing soon."

By midnight, the gin was beginning to wear off and with it her shallow ardor for Tres (maybe she didn't want him — with Stan so close in her thoughts — but Peg certainly didn't deserve to have him, either).

Suze left the ruckus in the library behind and went out into the great hall with its echoes and painted ceiling. She walked to and up the far staircase, her eyes adjusting to the darkness, and wandered the shadowy halls in the closed west wing. Most of the doors she tried were locked. Contractually, they were inhabiting only the east wing, but she was restless and starved for solitude, so she turned all the knobs until one opened. It was a long room overlooking the rear of the estate and the distant orchard of gnarled black tree trunks entreating the moon.

She sat on the sheet-shrouded daybed to drink in the quiet with her gin.

As her eyes began to adjust to the silvery light, dim objects in the room came into view: an ornate brass clock, uncovered, strangely; the legs of a mahogany dressing table visible under a sheet; a large painting on the wall facing the daybed.

Something about the picture gave her pause.

It was the necklace.

The woman in the portrait, whose features were partly painted over, had on the very necklace Suze now wore. The artist had captured its glint and rich waved contours well and crisply, and the likeness thrilled and terrified her.

The others seemed suddenly very far away indeed. Before she broke from the main gathering, she'd looked in on the band, which had broken for chow and spilled into the kitchen with bow ties askew and pressed white shirts coming untucked. Craving their easy banter now, she stood abruptly, then raced down the hall and down the steps with her empty glass. The band was with the others in the library, someone told her, so she headed back that way and almost ran smack into Tres, lolling in the hallway, smoking, alone.

He caught her lightly by the wrist, stabbing out his cigarette in a glass on the sideboard, and spun her over to him like a clumsy dancer. This might have charmed her under other circumstances, at least for a minute, but she felt too unnerved and tired to join in or even protest.

She closed her eyes and pretended his shirt was Stan's, that she could rest against his breastbone, and for a minute this strange boy was silent and let her, something Suze felt more than naturally grateful for. "You'll have to come back," she whispered, pulling away lightly, "and play some other day. I'm calling it a night." She motioned with her chin, her hair falling at a slant down her cheek. "And they don't know it yet, but they are, too."

"I'll do that." Tres smiled with only half as much guile as she was used to.

"Good."

He wasn't Stan, but she could pretend. Suze kissed him good night. Just because. And she almost meant it.

Tres didn't come to the next soiree, and she allowed herself a small dose of disappointment. She wandered about feeling adrift, unreal, lonely. Suze stood in a noisy corner with her eyes closed, swaying, and could almost feel Stan's hands strong in her hair, moving fast under her raccoon coat in the roadster.

She remembered the act of dressing for him to undress her: turned-down hose and powdered knees, scarlet screen-star lips like Clara Bow's, painting her mouth small and pert and bee-stung. Dressing for him had given her life meaning, ritual. She was a package for him to open. That was her gift to Stan, and she gave it over and over, and now she had his child inside her to show for it, was carrying his breath and blood in her body, and she would maybe never speak to him again. He would never know. And whom could she tell? Not Daddy or Emily. Damn Emily.

The one time she'd tried to tell her, they were visiting the residence hall at Wellesley that would become their new home in the fall. The need to tell someone was pressing so hard, Suze wondered if the baby hadn't become a mind, grown beyond its mere two-month shape, taking her over from within. Despite Emily's grouchy ranting about marriage and the college marriage market, Suze took solace in her own eyes in the powder room mirror and began to shape her announcement. "Stan," she said, because it all began there, didn't it? It began with Stan.

But she hardly got his name out.

"Oh, get over him, Suze." Dour Emily rolled her eyes. "He's done nothing but lead you on and leave you at the curb. If this is what it means to be in love, then hang love." She smacked her just-rouged lips and pinched her cheeks to color them, as if her appearance mattered to anyone. "Love undoes you," she badgered.

"Love makes you different. Makes you weak. You used to be a real person. I used to be able to talk to you."

Had Suze expected mercy?

"Now you make me sick."

Suze had felt the sting of this rant on two levels. Eager to be relieved of her secret, she had also let down her guard, left herself open to Emily's envy. It was weak, and it was thoughtless, and she felt something inside close to Emily forever. Perhaps it was the place the baby now inhabited. Private knowledge she as a woman had been initiated into and Emily had not, and couldn't fathom, much less sympathize with.

Repairing the grave arch of her brows with a twee-zers from her handbag, Suze had countered, "You've always been a little sickly, Emily, with your chills and sniffles and meek ways. A little *wet*, you know." Suze snapped her compact closed. "You're all wet. So get out and find someone else to rain on."

It began to rain on Wednesday, and by the time Daddy departed again and the weekend parties could begin, the moat was swollen, and the vast, sculpted lawn was a swamp.

Suze had not told Daddy about the mean man in the garden any more than she had told him about Tres or the others, the worldly and parasitic array that always knew when to show up and usually had the money to blend in. For all her father knew, it was just Suze and Peg, playing croquet on the big lawn and sipping lemonade.

When the crowd began to merge into one form, a screaming harpy in beads and tweed, she whispered to Tres, "Let me show you my favorite room in the house."

"Oh? Why your favorite?"

"It's quiet and looks out on the back patio. It feels a little haunted somehow. I've never had the nerve to go in daylight. When I wasn't drunk."

He reached into the fray for a passing bottle and topped off her champagne. "Well, don't let's break with tradition now."

They toasted, drank, drifted apart from the others. Their heels made no sound, even when the music became muted and distant, when the laughter came in traces.

When they reached the room and slipped inside, Suze asked, "So whatever happened to that princess? In that story of yours?" Tracing Tres's ear with her tongue, she led him to the daybed under the darkened portrait of the woman in the necklace. She had come to think of it as *her* necklace.

" 'If you truly love me,' the stranger said"—Tres stroked her bare neck—for mindful of Daddy's warnings, she had thought to remove the treasure and place it in a drawer before she got too drunk. Hidden it. It was one thing to pretend Tres was Stan while he was kissing her, but did she trust this local boy? She did not. She let her sable stole fall as he began to recite his folktale, the rain making light music on the old-fashioned lead windows, a slanting in the wind.

Conjuring Stan was something she did often, at the petting parties her older college friends had invited her to and later at her own parties. (*She's the* queen *of parties*, blowhard Peg always said.)

"'. . . if you love me, you will make me a gift'"— Tres yanked the dusty sheet off the daybed—"'of the silver key that unlocks the gates of the sea.'"

Suze let her dress fall round her ankles, and with her eyes closed, she could almost conjure it, the smell and feel of Stan's skin, the veins in his wrists as he smoothed the hanging hair from her face. The cushions were a silky chill beneath her back, and his weight a warmth. There was no moon tonight, and she could make out nothing in the painting, though she knew it was there.

Tres settled alongside her, lean and whispering. "'No!' said Dahut. 'Impossible!' Her father kept the key day and night on a chain round his neck, but the prince swore that if she got him the key, he would spirit her away to his kingdom of riches, where she would reign as queen. That night, she crept into her father's chamber. As the old king slept, she sneaked the key from his neck and returned with it to her lover.

"'Here is the key,' Dahut said. 'Let us leave.' But the prince was silent. He snatched it from her and went from the palace laughing, for he was the Devil in disguise—"

"Are *you* the Devil?"

Tres kissed her neck, and it was Stan's kiss. Stan's whisper. "Don't interrupt," he breathed. "Dahut watched her prince throw open the gates. There was a great creaking and tearing sound as seawater began to surge and curl through the sleeping city—"

"You really like this story, don't you?" Suze slurred, and he nibbled her fingers gently as he whispered, and she could hardly keep her eyes open.

"To this day, fishermen docked in Douarnenez on misty mornings hear the sound of church bells in the sea below, calling the faithful. If ever a sailor answers, it's said, the lost city of Ker-Ys will bob above the waves and become capital of all France. There's a Breton proverb: *Pa veuzo Paris, e tiveuzo Ker-Ys*—'When Paris shall sink, Ker-Ys shall emerge.'"

She shuddered for effect, but ended up giggling.

O let us be married! Too long have we tarried:
But what shall we do for a ring?

She giggled and giggled and curled up like a little sea-swept shrimp, exhausted, with her head reeling and the rain a lullaby.

Suze woke near dawn with a stain on her memory, hung over, and it took some time to orient herself. Sunday. Kerfol. The east wing. She sat up abruptly. In daylight, green eyes looked down at her.

My eyes.

The face in the painting was her face.

Suze wrestled her way out of the sheet and stood, queasy and reeling, strangely modest all of a sudden.

She groped her stole from the back of a chair, flung it over her shoulders, and went forth with hand extended as if she might meet her image partway, as if the painting were a mirror and she might take her own hand and be led away to the little boat under the moon in the land where the Bong-tree grows, where Stan would be waiting, and they'd dance by the light of the moon, themoon, themoon.

The same moon out there now, setting over Kerfol. But her own frame in unfamiliar clothes, a stranger staring down with her face but as cold and distant as the moon, themoon, themoon was just too terrible. She turned to tell him, "I have to tell you . . . Stan, I have to tell you."

Something terrible.

Something wonderful.

The figure under the sheet lay very still, and for a moment Suze hesitated. As she lifted the fabric like a magician unveiling astonishment, it was not Stan beneath, welcoming and beloved; it was not even Tres, whose youthful close-shaved face she now recalled with desperate clarity; it was the hideous old impostor from the garden, leering, the man with the pointy beard and eyes like ice. She screamed and fell back on the floor, scrabbling sideways like a crab in a confusion of shadows, a black lunging, a pulse—within or without, at once—deafening, and the last thing she saw was her own face. Beautiful in that necklace.

When I Love You Best

1982

*T*HEIR TOUR GUIDE, JULIET, was breathy in all the right places, a master of the dramatic pause. The stories of this house intrigued her; that was clear, though she'd probably told them a hundred times to a hundred busloads of blue-haired ladies. Juliet seemed genuinely interested in what she was saying, which wasn't an easy thing, Meg understood. Why invest or reveal yourself when irony was safer? Sarcasm. That was *Meg's* medium.

But Juliet's grace and confidence were eliciting a sort of grudging respect in Meg. The eyes of nearly everyone in their larger group followed their fearless leader across the shocking, unnatural green of the manor lawn. She was leggy and navigated the hedges and squishy grass cranelike, steps high and slow and elegant in stylish heels.

Their picnic blankets made of the vast lawn a bright, unfinished crazy quilt, and Juliet paused by each smaller group, speaking sometimes in English, sometimes French or German. There was a Japanese couple who may have felt slighted, but Juliet had a knack for making everyone feel special and at ease, even the uptight widow from Boston, who was too polite to play the token ugly American.

That must be me, Meg thought, picking at the boxed lunch of chunky bread and cheese, dried ham, and oily olives that had come with their ticket price. The plain white boxes had filled the far rear seat in the van in two teetering piles, and since she and Nick weren't speaking, Meg had spent most of the ride speculating about lunch. The real draw of the French countryside—or the Spanish or Italian, for that matter—was food, and she and Nick spent the better part of each day strategizing their next meal. How middle-aged was that?

Well, they had money to burn, thanks to Nick's parents, who wanted the Promising One to enjoy this post-graduation summer for all it was worth, get freedom out of his system. Get Meg out of his system, too, maybe. Lila would cheer that, Meg knew, though Nick's mother was too proper to say it outright.

"Like the baron's, Susanna Cole's murder was never solved," Juliet was saying. "They found her floating in the moat the next morning—you'll see when we walk around that it's long since been drained. Police were baffled by strange holes and mounds that had appeared all over the grounds in the night, as if every rabbit in France had gone to work on the property."

Meg laughed along with the others, though she wasn't sure what they were laughing *at*. Was that funny? Weird, yes, and probably false, but funny?

"The necklace that had very likely strangled her was never found, though a boy in the village, a suspect, confessed to trying to steal the piece. Something frightened him badly before he could get out with it. In the end, there was little viable evidence, forensic or otherwise." The wards of the estate had issued a reward for the necklace, Juliet explained, which as far as she knew was still on offer.

In halting English, the Japanese man said that he would keep his eyes peeled. He enjoyed the phrase so much that everyone laughed.

There was another, larger English-speaking group on the blanket beside theirs, so Juliet hovered between them awhile, trying to meet each tourist's eyes without making anyone ill at ease. Another of her many talents. "So together with his grief and the need to conceal from the press that his murdered daughter was also pregnant," Juliet said, her gaze sluicing over Nick like water, "Jack Cole had the embarrassment of the missing necklace, which he'd removed from a safe he was given access to in the master bedroom."

She glided away across the lawn again, all European grace and Chanel No. 5, to repeat her spiel in German. The name was pretentious—what parents in their right mind named their kid after a character in a play who stabs herself to death? But she spoke *at least* four languages, Meg had noted. Nick must have noticed, too. Juliet was not only good-looking; she was also polished and well bred. She was wearing stockings, for Christ's sake, and classy Italian shoes on this swampy lawn, which was the only maintained thing about this spook house. And let's not forget, she had the good sense and smarts to be working for an historical society in the first place, even if her job was telling sensationalized ghost stories to stupid tourists.

Meg might have earned a scholarship to Berkeley, where she and Nick were both heading in the fall, but she'd felt worse than stupid this entire trip, as if her mind had wandered out of range. When you got right down to it, she'd rather be in Amsterdam, getting stoned, or drinking margaritas in Tijuana. She wasn't ready for this. For college and couplehood and real life. Maybe it was Nick she (suddenly) wasn't ready for. Clever, charming Nick, who'd recrafted her application essays and cover letters to get her accepted to *not just any college,* but the right one. A good one. So they could be together. Little adults, Ethan would say.

Ethan, who was not skulking around the French countryside with a tour bus full of old ladies, but probably at a bullfight or drinking sherry in some tapas bar in Spain by now. No, not sherry. Beer. Bad, watery American beer, probably. Sherry would be too much like a grown-up. A little adult, yes, which *was* more and more what Meg felt like.

Come to think of it, Nick hadn't spoken to her *in*

any language for almost twenty-four hours—a cold war she only half-remembered the origins of—and she was tired of trying to meet his eye, of how attentive he was to everyone but her.

Was it just this feeling of being alone in a foreign land with no language, next-to-no money of her own, and Nick being a dick—all imperious and mature— that was bothering her? Nick the Dick, she might have joked back home, but not here. Not now, when a rift had ripped so splendidly between them—splendidly because underneath lived a pulse, surprising and shameful: *freedom.* It was not Ethan's voice, though it had to be his favorite word. How long had it taken her to figure that out? A week in Europe? Six days? Did it surprise her? The last time she'd seen Nick's twin, home in L.A. sophomore year, he was being shipped off to their father's old boarding school in England. How do you get expelled from public school in California?

Everyone stood to resume the tour as Juliet circulated a trash bag, but Meg hung back. That house was oppressive in a way she couldn't explain, the way storm clouds are oppressive, but she was *supposed* to feel that way about it. That was the point, which made her feel manipulated, which annoyed her even more.

When that German guy at the hostel mentioned Kerfol the day before, it had sounded fun in a Halloween-hayride sort of way, though she scoffed when Nick fished the listing from his *Road Less Taken* guidebook. This trip had made her cruel. But maybe she'd been right to resist coming. She sensed it right away, how hollow and bleak Kerfol was; the avenue in had seemed a gray tunnel leading further into their silence.

She had wanted to tell him something Friday night in that quiet vineyard row under the moon, and he had wanted to ask. The wanting hung between them like a blade, and for every glass of wine Nick refused, Meg had two. By the time he was ready to talk, she could barely stand up and was crooning about moonlight and screaming some Patti Smith song. Maybe he'd laughed at her, with her, and maybe he hadn't. That part of the night was lost. Erased. Meg didn't even know how they got back to the hostel and into those colorless, cold sheets, though she did remember reeling at the edge of their narrow cot-bed with Nick's arm limp over her collarbone, vomit pressing up from some fathomless emptiness inside her.

I have to ask, he had said. *I have to ask you something.*

"Don't speak," she'd roared back, playfully holding a palm up in front of Nick's face. Because *she* had something to say. Something unspeakable. It would change everything for him. For her, it already had.

So she'd been nervous, drunk too much wine, though she never drank. Nick thought it was stupid the way kids their age got loaded as if that were an end in itself. The strong vineyard wine had gone straight to her head, and they'd headed back to the hostel with her wobbling and lurching, colliding with his crisp white shirt. The bone in her nose bending on his collarbone, that smooth rise she loved to trace with her fingers, her stinging nose and the sudden smell of him, a woody soap smell, taming all her complaints. Taming her. How did he keep his shirts so crisp on the road in hostels and rented rooms? He put up with uncertainty for her sake, but before you knew it, he'd have his degree and a network to the perfect position at a socially conscious nonprofit that would also pay. Wasn't that the plan?

There was always a plan.

He would have let her kiss him, Meg knew, even in that state. Even reeking and senseless. He had dignity and grand intentions—more than any guy she'd ever known, and she'd known a few—but she could still disable all that with a simple, catlike rise and press of breast against his shoulder blade. She brought it out in him, the worst, and that was the best part of her power, the only reason she could hold her head up in his company. Nick was too good for her, and she knew it, and how could she forgive that?

Sometimes, young as they were, they seemed like some old couple on a park bench, chained ankle to ankle by habit. On the other hand, she hoped never to be as free as Ethan. As carefree.

Juliet led them inside and into what she called the west wing, her voice echoing under high ceilings. The checkered wood floors had been recently waxed and reflected a phantom procession in bright tourist clothes. The great hall, as Juliet called it, was full of furniture draped

in dusty cloth, and Meg sighed in the face of more rel-
ics. This trip was as much Nick's graduation present
to her as his parents' to him, since she had no money
to pay for it, but whose idea was this ruin rising out of
the ground like a stone ogre? And these dusty cloths?
Wasn't this trip supposed to be about beginnings? Why
didn't they just end the cold war, shove and shriek and
end up a tangle of tongue and raw hairline? Nick had it
in him to do that. Never mind his bad-boy twin — Nick
had his own dark side, his own wildness, Meg knew,
but it was bleak and private, like the moors near where
he and Ethan had grown up in the north of England.

Nick hated to show this side, admit to it even, but
Meg knew it was there. She knew how to access it. It
was what attracted him to her, despite their obvious
incompatibility where most everything else was concerned. They had a good raw, physical attraction, but
only when she pushed him. Pushed him.

Juliet's voice droned on, but Meg had focused on
the music. Somebody was playing a radio far off, either
some historian up in another wing of the house or
some neighbor out in the countryside. She imagined a
carload of lanky Breton boys heading home from the
beach with tans and a cooler in the backseat. How did
she get invited on *that* field trip?

With a dramatic sweep of her arm, Juliet pulled a
sheet off a large gilt-framed painting, and Meg snapped
to. Susanna Cole. There was the necklace Juliet kept
talking about, though no flapper hairstyle. No beads.

And what about the pout you'd expect from a poor little rich girl in exile? The one in the picture looked like she'd lived centuries ago, not as recently as 1926. Meg thought to ask this question, but refrained when she noticed Nick's shoulder touching the tour guide's. He was drawn in, standing close to see what she unveiled next.

"Curators have tried to identify the artist with no luck. The painting was damaged when they found it in the attic back around the turn of the last century. Layered over. They had to scrape down and restore the image underneath." She reached out. "You can still see a bit of the red paint here. And here."

After they'd all had a good ponder, Juliet covered the painting again and led them up a staircase, turning back to Nick. "A minor or at least unknown artist, and the same one . . ."

The group followed into a small anteroom. ". . . who did the handsome drawing of Anne de Barrigan hanging over that desk."

Nick peered up at the faded color sketch in a simple frame.

"She looks sad," he whispered when Meg arrived by him.

She felt her eyes tear up involuntarily. It was the first real thing he'd said to her all day, apart from where to, and how much, and what time. Maybe he wasn't addressing her at all, but the group, himself, the air. For the rest of the tour, Meg hardly registered anything except that she was tired and her head hurt and she wanted a cup of coffee, nothing fancy. Just comforting. Dunkin' Donuts.

They lingered in the baron's chamber, which had French doors overlooking a courtyard. While the others tuned in to the spiel, Meg looked out at the sun playing off cracked urns and overgrown roses and longed to be out there with her face raised to the sun. What she most wanted was a cigarette. But Nick would kill her if he knew she'd taken one from Ethan before they all went their separate ways at the hostel that morning. Whenever she had a moment to herself, she fished out the bent cigarette to breathe the sweet smell of tobacco, and it reminded her, and made her ashamed again, and she stowed it away once more in her backpack.

The baron's room was large, imposing, dark in the corners, so she kept by those French doors and watched butterflies inspect the half-restored garden in the courtyard. She studied the orchards beyond, fruit trees with their distorted limbs.

Finally it was time to go.

They had pondered the last ancient object, heard the last bloody spook tale, clutched tight the last waxy banister. The last old lady had ducked out under the servants' exit at the rear of the house, and Juliet had eased the door closed on its rusty hinges and snapped the decayed lock into place. They were allowed to stand in the sun and contemplate the grounds from the rear of the estate—the stables and abandoned dovecote, the distant chapel.

Nick stood alone by a trellis that was sinking into the earth and swallowed in vines. Meg walked over, took a breath for courage, and hugged him from behind, hugged him in that nervous, goofy way she used to when they first met back in the seventh grade and she had to hold him still, had to have that subtle, restless energy in her arms without the responsibility of facing it head on.

"We should come back," she told the nape of his neck, a challenge, a plea. "At night. When no one's here. *Really* get off the beaten path. . . ."

When he didn't reply, she whispered suggestively, "I'm bored, Nick."

"We should catch up," he said. The others had followed in single file across and alongside the moat circling the building.

"Are you scared?" she asked his back, the beautiful, lean curve of that back. *Why do I love you best when you're walking away from me?*

He turned and smiled at her, and the smile hurt like a fall on the ice, like the palms of your hands skidding across the ice. Meg had been a champion skater once. She had played with dolls. She had dreamed of coming to France. She had known Nick. She had always known Nick, it seemed.

"Of course I'm scared, you idiot."

She smiled back at him.

"Is that what you really want?" he accused. "We're supposed to be having fun, you know. Will that make this trip fun for you?"

She nodded eagerly, feeling a wave of guilt, for maybe she just wanted to compare notes with Ethan later, wanted something daring to show for herself, something stupid and reckless that would impress him. Why did it matter now, impressing Ethan, when it never had before? What had changed?

"And you'll stop sulking?"

She nodded, subdued now, solemn. Did he know? Did Nick know? He had to know. Why else the long morning's silence? The sun was low. The stones of that dismal house cupped each creeping shadow.

"I will. I promise."

He smiled and leaned into her, and she spoke softly into the clean-smelling linen of his shirt, and for the moment, just a moment, Meg was grateful. "I just know you've always wanted to do it in a haunted house." She reached around and flicked his nose. "Haven't you?"

When the van parked, Meg let Nick thank Juliet on behalf of them both. She had nothing to say to someone like that. Even, "Thank you . . . Good-bye," seemed too tiring. They didn't check back at the hostel. It was their last night in Brittany, and they had nothing to lose. Nick called to have them hold their bags until the next day; they'd fetch them and head directly to the train station.

They had the taxi set them down at dusk at a nearby crossroads. No point drawing attention to themselves. They'd just reached the entrance to Kerfol when the sun vanished like something hurtling down a well. The dark took Meg's breath. She reached absently for Nick's hand, and they dragged their feet until their eyes adjusted, proud when it happened, as if it initiated them into some secret club: We Who See in Darkness. There was a thin, fogged moon, but the night was overcast.

They hurried. Laughing. Nervy. Meg tried not to imagine the creatures out there in the dark. Were there bears in Brittany? Wolves? What? She should have paid attention more during the tour.

The night was windless, soundless.

Meg found a brick-size rock and began to smash at the rusty lock on the rear servants' door.

"What about alarms?" Nick stood back, wary. He winced at the noise, so fierce in the silence.

"We'll find out, but I doubt it. Look around." She shrugged. "There's no money to fix anything. Isn't that why all these old noble families are renting their places out for tours anyway?"

The lock snapped and spun a moment, swinging to a stop. And now the stillness felt accusatory.

Inside the building, Meg could barely breathe for the excitement of it all: the hollow chill of the rooms, the humped shadowy shapes that she knew were sheets, the shifting and squeaking of their rubber soles. The occasional far-off music that today had sounded like radio now seemed to be issuing from the attic, and she was too terrified to wonder, too excited to stand still. A kind of restless energy burned through her. All she could think to do, to calm her nerves and make the next eight hours — which she had insisted upon — bearable, to salvage them and find her strength, was to seize Nick's hand and draw him up the stairs.

She knew the big room at the top, the baron's chamber, had a bed in it still, though perhaps no top mattress or bedclothes. At least they could lie down; he could lay her down and kiss her fear away, and they could be young again. They did, and he did, and it was as sweet as it had been in a long time, not stormy and rough, as it sometimes was these days with one or the other of them withholding or punishing or playing indifferent, and she slept sweetly in Nick's arms, dear Nick, familiar Nick, who hardly said a word but let her have this night as if it were the last gift he could give her.

The sound of some animal in the night woke them. Just a brief yip, almost a bark. "A fox, maybe," whispered Nick. They lay a long time in the silence, poised for more, but as the silence wore on, they drifted off again, too groggy and edgy to speak of it, to break the protective spell of sleep.

But then Meg heard it again, intruding into a restless dream. A single, mournful yowl. She sat up in bed, aware now as she hadn't been before of the dusty smell of the top sheet, shaking Nick.

"Go look?"

He snorted. "Yeah, sure. I'll just mosey out and get my throat cut like every idiotic white boy in every slasher movie ever made. Thank you, no."

"Thank you, no," she mimicked, snidely. "There's that noise again."

"Feral dogs," Nick offered. "They probably live out behind the chapel and the orchards. I saw woods and fields back there. I'll bet they smelled the trash from our lunch today. I didn't see Juliet put it in the van, did you? Maybe there's a Dumpster out back or something."

Meg sat up, shivering, and put on her clothes, then burrowed back under the sheet with Nick.

The memory came so suddenly, and it was so present and unbearable, that she winced. She nuzzled his shoulder to feel his clean scent, but Nick climbed out of bed. He was walking toward the window and away. Now he was looking out as the memory surged over her like storm water over stones, like wrath. Did she imagine she could forget it, or spare Nick? Life didn't work that way.

He stood in the faint gray light of the window as the sound grew louder—there had to be a dozen or more dogs out there now, baying and barking—and it was the bleakest sound in the world, what made people in the Dark Ages fear the Big Bad Wolf, the sound of carnage past or carnage to come. "Do you see them out there?"

Nick's silence terrified her.

"Nick? Answer me—"

He only hushed her, drawing the ancient curtain closed but peering through a crack.

"What *is* it?"

"There's a man out there, too."

"Jesus Christ. You're messing with me. *Nick.*" She paused but couldn't bear the silence. "What man? Quit moving it!"

Nick was still fussing with the curtain, drawing attention to them.

"What *man?*" She threw a pillow to stop him from advertising, but he lifted the other arm to block it.

"I almost thought for a minute that it was Ethan."

Was he joking? "I guess I deserve it since this was my stupid idea." Was that supposed to be a joke? "But you *are* messing with me, right?"

"He's wearing a costume or something. Ethan would do that. He likes drama, doesn't he?"

Nick looked back at her, and she was glad he couldn't see her eyes. Couldn't read her face.

"I thought maybe it's some local kid playing a prank, but it *could* be my brother. Couldn't it?" Nick let the curtain fall. He came and knelt by her. "Did you tell him we'd be here, and this is some trick to screw with poor Nick? Because I'm all set with that."

She shook her head, desperately. "Of course not!"

"I don't like this stuff, and you both know it."

Both? "So why'd you bring us here in the first place?"

Oblivious to the stranger outside, the baying dogs, the terror that had stopped her blood and cast everything into perspective—terrible, jagged, real—he snarled, "*I* brought us here? Me?"

"It was your idea to come," she insisted. "The first time." *Nick,* please. "Stop looking at me like that—"

"Like what?"

"Like that—"

He grabbed her chin and held it hard, painfully. "Is that Ethan out there screwing with me?"

No. She shook her head, mostly to get out of his grasp. "No, Nick."

He slumped and laid his cheek on the bed beside her, like someone too tired to move, and now his voice sounded muffled, far away. "Maybe you wish it was, though, Megs? Maybe you'd rather be here with Ethan—"

She kicked off the sheet, stood up, and pushed past him to the window. The dogs, wherever they were, had fallen quiet. "This isn't the time," she reminded him, drawing the curtain aside a hair. An inch. Enough to see what Nick had seen, the figure of a dark-haired young man in tights and short pants and a white, puffy movie-pirate shirt. A costume. He was tall and lean like Ethan (and Nick). But not like. It was too dark to really see his face, but he stood so still, and looked up so attentively, that she shuddered. She almost pitied him. What did he want? Whatever it was, he wanted it bad. What was *he* seeing?

"Nick—"

But Nick wasn't there. Not on the bed or beside it or anywhere. She called his name as if he were her child and she'd lost him in the mall, then stood with a hand over her mouth, regretting it. Ridiculous. She noticed a candleholder with a crooked stump on it, snatched it off the mantle, and dug in the pocket of her jeans for matches. Ethan had given her the matches, too. She fumbled, feeling the broken cigarette, the tobacco on her fingers, but no matches.

At last she found them, struck and struck again. The candle flared up blue, then settled into a white flame with a blue center, like a narcissus. Is that the flower? Jesus. She was thinking about flowers. Flowers made her think about funerals. Meg winced at the new, leaping shadows.

Then Nick was in the doorway, looking gaunt and strange. He was holding up a hand mirror, a woman's mirror with tarnished metalwork on the handle. "Look at yourself," he ordered. "Look." He crowded her back against the wall beside the glass doors, and the heavy curtain bumped her candle. The light wavered, and the candle fell, rolling out of view. It was dark again, and she couldn't see his face.

"Look at *what*? I can't see you, Nick. Don't do that. Get *off* me."

Though his body was weirdly rigid and apart, he'd laid his head on her shoulder. He was mouthing something against her shoulder, his cheek resting heavy against her shoulder bone. Only that cheek and his faint movements alerted her that he was there, that close, and she felt her own sadness welling up, rearing up like a sea monster from the dark.

"I tried to tell you—"

He was crying. She couldn't stand that. It made her sick.

"Say it."

"Nick," she gasped. "You have to stop." She wanted to hurt him. *Make it stop.* She shoved him back, and while his hands and arms and torso remained apart, stiff as a tree, his head stayed on her shoulder, attached to her like one of those wretched Siamese twins who have to eat and breathe and sleep and raise their children together because their flesh rules—helpless as a clamp, a trap.

"Say it—" He was a terrible, sobbing stranger and the person she knew best in the world. Well enough to know she couldn't hold him, couldn't make it better, though he might want her to, though she might want to. It was too late for that, and this made her angry. She pushed him again, hard this time, so he couldn't use her as a crutch anymore, couldn't lay his weight against her.

The dogs were at it again, near enough to the window to stop her heart, if she had a heart. *I have no heart.* He was somewhere else in the room now. She didn't know where.

"Say what you did."

"OK—" she began.

"Say it!" *Sayitsayitsayit.*

"I did. I'll say it. I did it with him, Nick."

He groaned, wherever he was, as if it hurt to hear it though he already knew, had known as soon as it happened, had maybe always known she wasn't good enough for him, not moral or mature enough.

"Go ahead. Get mad."

Make it stop.

"Do it, for once. Get mad. I want that," she wailed. "I want you to, Nick—you've earned it—but you might want to do it later, because there's someone *out there.*" Did she care? Could it matter now? "There's someone out there," Meg repeated, in a small, pathetic voice.

She felt him lunge, and she sprang out of the way, scrabbling for the candle, which was still and miraculously burning down low by the wall, but so were the curtains. She yanked one half of them down and tried to wave the fire out; she waved to keep it between them, too, as if there weren't enough between them already.

He stood up, and the knees of his khaki pants were black with something, stained. He lunged again, and in her panic she dropped the burning fabric, slipping in the same something—or was he pulling her down—slipping and scrabbling on a floor slick with blood, or another substance that smelled of salt and metal. Blood on his knees and palms, and they struggled, coughing, through the smoke toward the door, not together exactly but at once, and her own voice sounded wild as a bear. By the stairs Nick slipped again, and fell, thudding down in the dark.

She heard this, and then silence, and her fists clenched, and there were sirens. There was smoke.

Meg woke in a hospital. When her eyes opened, there was Nick, sitting in a chair beside her bed. No, not Nick.

While the two of them were still unconscious, one of the nurses had dialed the phone number scribbled on a train stub in Nick's wallet—Ethan's friend's apartment in Barcelona—the only contact info she could find on either of them.

"He's over there," Ethan assured her, hooking his thumb. "Boy genius is awake behind the curtain. But he's not speaking to me. He keeps rolling away like he has a stomachache. Might still be in pain, but Doc says he'll be fine. It's just a concussion and some bruises.

The shoulder's all popped in." Ethan gave hers a little knuckle-punch. "You guys are in some deep shit with the law. Who knew he had it in him? But he's fine."

Neatly folded on a plastic chair beyond his curtained bed was Nick's Oxford button-down, as crisp and clean as ever, apart from garish stripes of dirt from his fall down the staircase, like skid marks on a road. Bloodless.

"Right. Sorry to interrupt your holiday, big guy."

He laughed, licking his lips, and it wasn't a laugh she loved. It wasn't Nick's laugh, identical though they might seem. Identical in almost every way. "You oughta be sorry, kid. But as I say, he'll be fine."

Kid.

Was that what she was?

Ethan pulled a plastic baggie from the pocket of his denim jacket and started rolling a cigarette on the chair arm. Meg rolled away and off the pillow in disgust. She pressed her hot cheek against the lime-green hospital wall, and it felt cool and blank, like a blessing. She knew Nick would recover but that she would never see him again, that his brother would be forgiven, but she would not be. "Yes," she agreed, writing Nick's name, her best friend's name, on the wall with a bruised finger. "He'll be fine."

The Red of Berries

2006

D A CAN RANT ALL HE WANTS — "Gavin, this," and "Gavin, that" — when he's pissed, but he backs off when I fix him with a look. My Old Testament stare, he calls it, as in *I Will Smite Thee,* and let's hope it works on roofers.

I fired them today, his cronies, because Da's not here and I am.

Erik and Denez had just finished the burnt-out section of the west wing. Rebuilt and retiled the roof completely. Fine job, too, and Da thought to keep them on some, give them heavy lifting, stonework, what have you. But with him down for the count, I can't see spending another week on-site with these guys, much less the month or more the job will take. They're good with a hammer — and loyal to my da — but better at stuffing their mugs with their wives' lunches and trolling for porn on Erik's laptop. After a bit of that, they sit around smoking with Brie on their teeth and flicking their butts all over the new lawn I'm laying from seed. They've no use for a deaf seventeen-year-old boss. And I've no use, anymore, for them.

All the while I'm fighting to look them in the eye while I fire them, Clio's sprawled at my feet panting like the sweet, dumb mutt she is — her tongue a flapping flag of surrender.

"You're sure about that, Gavin?" Den can sign and knows it's easier for me. Almost all Da's friends can sign some — *because he says so.* But I also read lips, thanks to Mum, who thought I'd do better in the bigger world that way. "Bagad won't like it," Den adds regretfully.

"Yeah," Erik puts in. "Your father won't like it."

I breathe in, storing up for the garbled adventure that is speech, since Erik's not one of Da's that learned to sign. "He'll see my side." They don't wince, but you can see it in someone's face when you have to modulate, so I lower my voice. "I don't need you now. Too many cooks in the kitchen."

Den holds out his cell, but I pat my pocket. "It's all set," I lie. "He'll be in touch about the place in Normandy." I fish in the back pocket of my jeans for the postdated checks Da wrote. At breakfast, I penned in today's date and forged Da's initials. "Here."

They just stare at me, and I stare back.

I'm not brave, but I've never been especially afraid, either. I saw no use in fear once Mum died. The worst had happened. I don't have nightmares like my sister,

Sondra, does still, flailing and fussing about the dark. My mind's like still water, and most of the people in my life know not to cast stones into it.

"He's a mad little dog," Uncle Sean once spat, when I was eleven and nearly brained him with a shovel while we were digging Sondra's cat's grave and he unwittingly made her cry. "It's the runt quiet ones, not the big barkers, you have to worry about." He'd ducked just in time, and my uncle looked shaken, but he forgave me at once. I could see that. "They pounce, those quiet ones, and won't let go."

Finally Erik takes the check, his hand striking like a snake. Beady eyes search out the amount, and when he finds it, he sucks his teeth and shrugs. "So."

Den doesn't give in as easily, but in another minute Erik grabs the other check, too, spits on the ground, and nudges Den off toward the shuttered stables, where our trucks are parked.

I don't notice them drive away, but when Clio leaps up to chase them down the gravel and out through the gates onto the main avenue, I relax.

I don't wait for her to come back. She always does, good old girl, always comes when I whistle. We understand each other, and I'll never punish Clio with a leash unless she crosses me. I yawn and think about taking a nap. After a lot of cajoling from Da, the historical society agreed to let me board for the duration in the abandoned cottage at the far edge of the property, beyond the chapel, stables, dovecote, and the near-ruined orchard. The orchard is next on my list. There's no task I know more satisfying than pruning.

But before I can relax into that or anything else, I should text Da and fess up. He won't be pleased, especially that I advanced their full month's wages, but I've worked hard to prove that I'm capable of making this kind of decision.

There's no telling if he'll look at his text messages anytime soon. He isn't expecting to hear from me until the weekend. The insurance has been giving him hell on account of his back, and though Sondra squawked, we got rid of the landline to save money. The three of us are pretty good about texting.

As it turns out, there's no cell access anywhere on the grounds. Yesterday I had luck up by the road, but I'm not making that trek right now. I'll fetch supper later at the cybercafé in town and text from the road or e-mail Da when I get there.

As I say, I'm rarely afraid. Sondra says it's because I'm too logical, but a couple of weeks before I drove up here in Da's loaded flatbed from Quimper, I'm in the waiting room at the dentist's reading an article in a movie magazine. It's an interview with some Italian director, and he's going on about soundtracks, how a movie soundtrack can paint the mood for almost any scene. The drums tell the heart to beat. The strings set your nerves on edge. So I form this theory. Maybe I'm not afraid because my world is buffered by silence, sort of unspoiled.

I have no soundtrack, I guess you could say, but I remember music. I've only been deaf a few years. What's more, I come from a musical family. It's hard to be deaf in a family like ours, though no one, least not my Mum and Da, ever purposely made me feel the loss. But back when Mum was still with us, it shook the floors some nights, made the chair under me shiver. I could stomp along all right, but I'm no Beethoven and will always be off the rhythm, out of key.

But speaking of reception, it's funny that since I've been here, my inner ear, the one that works on memory—not vibration, as for others—has been on a tear. I keep hearing snatches of fiddle. Sean or Da would call it "violin," nose in the air; all three brothers play, or used to, the old-timey music, stomp-to reels and the sad old ballads, *gwerziou* and *sonniou* about drowned lovers and such. They fiddle.

This is a bleak, worked-up tune, gypsy-wild but also refined, repeating over and over, and I'm hearing it—or a memory of it—tuning in and out again all over the grounds, especially near the building.

My mind may be like still water, but sometimes a thing lights on it like a leaf, and there's this ripple, this storm of rings. That girl I thought I saw this morning behind the chapel, for instance, bending by a tangle of briars. This land is rich and overrun, and locals must find plenty to poach: rabbits, berries, whatever.

But this morning's trespasser seemed mystical, like a deer you meet on a path in the woods when you aren't hunting, aren't looking. She wasn't real, couldn't be real—she was dressed funny, for one thing, like an old-fashioned maid with pleated, poofy skirts, an apron, a little cap—so maybe I made her up to pass the time. She reminded me of that song Mum liked to sing. "She Moved Through the Fair," I think it was called. Now *there* was haunted—whether because Mum's gone now or just because she had the right voice for those lyrics—and Da accompanied so solemnly, sweetly, on his fiddle, as if to urge her gently toward the place where the song led. As if he saw the future.

Da more or less gave up his fiddle after Mum passed. "It's God's gift to you, man," my uncle Sean grumped. "You have to use it."

"You mean the same God that took my wife?" Da challenged. "And my son's hearing?" Sometimes even now he forgets I read lips. Or maybe Da wanted me to get that, wanted me to know what I'd cost him, what Mum had cost him, though he's never been spiteful that way.

"What song and why—if not for them?"

Sean winced and shook his head, pouring another cup of coffee for them both.

The not speaking seemed to physically weigh on them until Da said, "There, now. Shaddup, Sean," meaning go on and talk about football or some shop-woman's fabled backside, and my uncle obliged.

◆ ◆ ◆

So this music, it fades in and out, like cell-phone reception. The signal comes and goes depending where I stand. Do I remember this tune? Wouldn't I remember this tune? I have a little mental card catalog of stored music, a treasury I draw from without warning. I can rarely call something up when I need it, but tunes come unannounced and knock me flat. Maybe this music is something I've heard, one of Mum's CDs — she wasn't hardened against "the violin" like Da and sometimes listened to old-guy composers with names like Ciconia or Corelli or What-Helly.

I'm worrying about Clio now and start whistling for her. What if she galloped into the road and under the wheels of a car? What if Den and Erik dognapped her for spite? She always comes when I call. Always.

I wait an agonizing while and then whistle again, loud, though of course I can't hear a thing; I just feel it, a wind in my ears, a storm in my head, and a few minutes later she blows past my legs at a canter, gleefully twisting in play. It's what she does when I walk her in the park and there are dogs there, when they run circles round each other, snapping and sniffing each other's rear ends. Only here there are no other dogs. It's sort of eerie and fascinating, something I've never seen her do before.

Clio tears past again, and I watch her curiously, sitting on a stone bench and fishing my cold egg-salad sandwich from the morning's wrinkled café bag, feeling the damp, and taking in the expanse of the grounds. It's a fine old place, despite how run down it's gotten; I can see why the historical society hired Da once they got their grant. He charges a fair deal more than some contractors but has a reputation for restoring, not just renovating. He's got the authentic eye, people say, and now I do as well, after years of early mornings, of Da giving the blanket and my rear a boot, and when I roll over, signing, "You can't quit, man. It's a family business." Sondra, who keeps the books, hears her version of same.

I do carpentry and stonework, but Da saw it was the green I do best. It's that shaping of the unruly natural world into something formed, the crafting over of chaos — never doing away with it, which is impossible, I know — but scissoring, snipping, molding. So at the ripe old age of fourteen or fifteen, I became the garden and landscape department of Da's "authentic" operation. He sent me to Versailles to study the gardens there. He advised long Sunday drives, said mind what the wealthy do in their gardens and why. He taught me devotion to and respect for what's humble: the worm, the bee, the frost. It's a modest life and it suits me, which is more than most sons-in-line-for-the-family-business can brag.

It's making me uneasy, Clio tearing up and down the lawn like she's in some sort of crowded dog park or something. They say animals and babies see angels and ghosts and whatnot, which makes me think of that girl again, her mouth stained bright with berry juice. After I stopped hearing, I found I still needed to use words hearing people take for granted, words like *loud,* only I used them about verbs or colors. The red on that girl's face was a "screaming" red.

Maybe Clio saw her, too.

Maybe she's seeing her still.

Like before, Clio's running and snapping at the ground like a doggie mime, and I don't like to admit it, but it looks like she's having fun *with others,* and it's making me seriously nervous.

People say this place is haunted. When my friends heard I was coming, they made the mock noose and the finger-slicing-the-neck and the bug eyes and said I'd be dragged into the homely bowels, never to be seen again. I was stoical about this. People say the same about a lot of the old houses, and forgive me, but my friends are dumb as dung. They're good guys, patient — those who stuck around after I lost my hearing even learned to sign a little — but a few clowns short of a circus.

I don't doubt it's haunted, but the grounds seem peaceful enough to me. Not kind or welcoming — nature isn't that, in my experience — just indifferent. But I've no ill will with the dead. When your own mum's dead, you don't.

For me, living in a hearing world's something like living in a world with ghosts anyway. Everyone's on the other side of a veil of silence, speaking mystery. They just are.

Clio's barking furiously. I don't hear this. I see it. When I go to investigate, I see she's been digging up chunks of my new lawn. I'm furious and confused—Clio's not a digger—and I point at the hole and kick it with my boot, and give her a little crack on the nose. "No," I say.

No.

Later, when I come looking for my water bottle, she's been at it again. Another crack on the nose. Another "No."

The next time I find a chunk of the lawn torn up, I leash her and tie her to one of the hedge boughs.

It doesn't stop, though. Those holes keep coming.

Rabbits, maybe.

What's more, when I look over at the tree where I've leashed Clio, I see she's up on her haunches, barking. I worry she'll choke herself, and I have the shit-poor feeling I'm missing something; something's happening just out of earshot. I'm missing out on the soundtrack that's there whether I like it or not, whether I hear it or not.

But the funny thing is, I do. Hear something. Things—around here. That, or the weirdness of being alone on a remote property, is making me remember old soundtracks from days past, when I could hear. A lifetime ago.

Either way, Clio's not my digger, so I untie her,

and the minute I do, she goes tearing back out toward the chapel. I follow, and sure enough, there's the girl in the funny clothes, gathering berries like before, like she never left, her lovely lips stained red in a too-pale face. I don't see Clio, but I know she's out here somewhere, barking and making a to-do.

"Wait," I call out, a little desperate, which makes me feel like I'm in school, in the hallway, trying to catch a girl's eye while she preens at her locker, and I hate that feeling, hate being that kid with what feels like bread caught in my throat, words backing up. I don't know why it should matter when everyone in my school is deaf like me. But there's always something to feel wrong about.

She's probably scared of me by now. Like a deer. Scared off. "Stay there," I whisper, not wanting to startle her with my garbled words. I raise a finger. *Wait.* "Please."

She looks as if she wants to speak, so I wait, and she says one word — I can only tell because her lips seem to exaggerate the word for my sake, the way kindly people sometimes try to overenunciate when they realize I'm deaf, until I take out my notepad and write down what it is I'm trying to say — her eyes downcast, trained on her raised apron front.

Hungry.

I could hit her with a stone, but I can't reach her in any straightforward way. The bridge crossing is nailed over — and the boards rotted, probably — but

I can circle back and cross at the ornamental bridge downstream. When I get back, digging into my pocket for notebook and pen, she stands looking for all the world as if she knows me. She reaches up and almost touches my unwashed hair. All of a sudden I feel shy and self-conscious. Dirty. Ugly. Because she isn't. Not at all.

"Youen," she says, tilting her head, and her wide gray eyes are sad and sort of tender, so I start blushing. Maybe she's retarded or has amnesia, like in the movies. But I don't think so. I don't know what to think. I feel like I do when I drink too much coffee on a job with Da and start to shake a little and my head's racing.

Youen.

I heard that.

I heard her say it.

I shake my head, struggling to keep the words back in my throat, not to pummel her with them, and scribble on a piece of paper. *My name's Gavin. I'm deaf, and it's hard for me to form words without yelling.*

She looks confused, so I smile, and write, *I don't want to yell at you. You look like you'll run away again.*

She looks blank and shakes her head again, smiling back at me.

I write, *Where do you come from?*

Her white fingers trail lightly over my handwriting, not quite touching the page, and she shakes her head again, hard.

"You can't read?"

She smiles at me with her eyes, and they slip past me.

I turn and see Clio barking behind me. She races forward and my girl retreats into the woods. Clio comes back wet and shivering.

"Jesus." I coax her over and grab her collar, frayed red canvas with black-and-white musical notes, something Mum chose; it was as old as Clio, nearly. "Look what you've done now." I drag Clio off into the house. We're both breathing hard, and she's pacing, sniffing the floor, bounding up the steps.

I have a key to the west wing, the formerly burned-out side, and since we came I've explored some in there, as anyone would. Sometimes I snoop under the dusty coverings or just sit and imagine the rooms as they were once. I do this a lot. We work on a fair number of historic properties, and I like the past, the legends and family histories. Even now, with Clio leaping frantically at one of the doors at the top of the staircase, I pause to scan a sign the historical society put up. About some seventeenth-century murder involving dogs.

Dogs, plural.

That's bad enough, but nothing compared to what happens next. Spooked good now and not caring if I attract or amuse distant neighbors, who are probably used to this and laughing over their bouillabaisse, I shout for Clio, then begin bounding up the stairs after her when I collide with something clammy. It feels a lot like the time I ran under Gran's wash line as a boy, chasing a ball, and the wind slapped a bedsheet at me. The damp fabric molded to my face and chest, and I felt a sort of breathless panic. When you get unpeeled again and free, you feel a bit silly, but before that, before you know what it is and what it isn't, there's that bad suffocating feeling. It's how I feel on that stairwell, not hurt or horrified, just *clung* to and confused. I turn and glimpse a tall figure, a gliding light, fleeing down the stairs, faint and shaped like a woman.

And then it's gone. Just like that. And the world is black, and I'm shivering on the stairwell with Clio upstairs somewhere. The light is utterly gone — because the sun set when I wasn't looking.

The cavernous house, which should be quiet, as all things are for me, is creaking and heaving down low, like a living thing, something large and sluggish waking up. I breathe deep, searching for stillness in my mind.

I can't get out of here, I think, *won't get out of here, if I don't make my mind lie down again.*

"Clio!" I bark, and she bounds past me. We take the rest of the stairs in twos and threes, though I keep a good hold on the banister. We blow through the door and out toward the stables, where the truck's parked.

She jumps right in, trembling the way only a dog can tremble, and I'm right after, but of course the truck won't start. Ridiculous, sure, to think an engine will start at a time like this. I beat my head against the wheel as the trees in the orchard raise their shadowy arms in benediction against the last line of an overcast sunset.

I keep right on knocking my forehead against the steering wheel, trying to get back to sense, trying to get my wits about me, but I don't. I can't. I reach back and drag Clio close by the collar. It's probably just the battery, in which case I'll flag down a car from up the main road and get a jump.

The last dull glow beyond the trees is going, and I wonder where I left my flashlight, and how the hell I'm going to find my way up to the road without a moon. This place is nowhere and anything but silent. I can't hear Clio whimpering, though I feel her throat vibrating against my leg. I knead her fur and murmur as best I can and don't dare open the car door, for what I hear out there is madness. I'm getting that it's the same scene, happening over and over, and that mostly I'm hearing it. A loop. The violin, loud and then fading. A rabble of dogs. A woman's scream. Repeating, like the refrain in a song.

I'm hearing it.

And I'm sure as shit I don't want a new verse to start.

Clio hears my soundtrack, too. I can tell. She's sniffing and straining and cowering, and I train my gaze on that side of the house and spot a guy in a white shirt in the courtyard, and for no reason I can name, this gives me hope, though I can't imagine why it should. Except that I'm an optimist. I let Clio out but hold her tight on the leash, though she strains. I call to the man and approach hesitantly.

Maybe it's Erik, I think, *or Den, back to check up on me or give me a scare.* But he looks younger, slender and tall, maybe some teenager checking out the house on a dare, and this is even more hopeful. He's probably as spooked as I am. "Hey!" I warble, not worrying how loud. "Hey—where are you parked? I . . . need . . . a . . . jump."

And then the man turns around. I get a good look at him—more funny clothes, breeches for threads and what-have-you—just as Clio rips the leash out of my hand and goes tearing between the geometric hedges like a rodeo horse careening around barrels. She leaps at him, leaps on him, through him, but the figure only turns solemnly back to the window, unfazed. The upstairs window.

Jesus H. Christ.

I begin to run for the wall. I scale it, whistling for Clio, crash through briars and thick wisteria vines, and I'm not looking at this point, believe me, but I've found that girl again. She's standing by a stone bench, looking different from the other devilry around here and about as forlorn anyone can. She's trying to say something, her mouth is moving, and it's a beautiful mouth, and her hair's falling loose and wild from a bonnet—I can't believe I even know what that's called, but I do; must be all the signs I've read in all these old houses—and I can see the white flesh above her dress where the dress pushes her breasts up, and the white throat, and she steps forward with an outstretched hand, and I can't believe that I nearly let her take my hand, but then I think better of it and feel like reaching out instead to smooth the tears from her eyes, but she's shaking her head, shaking and shaking it as if for all the world her heart will break, and I think of my mum, dead in heaven, and I think of this girl, dead but here, and I wonder what anyone could do to help her—I wish my mother could, or someone, because this girl is so obviously trying to help me, and weird as life is right now, I really want to put my arms around her until she calms down, or maybe doesn't calm down, or else calms me down, and now I'm thinking I must be a freak with a death fetish or something, but she's so pretty, so sad, and I sort of trust her when I see that Clio trusts her. What else is there to trust?

When she starts backing away toward the avenue—at least I think it's toward the avenue; it's too dark to tell; toward the trees anyway—I go that way, too. But in a minute I sense that I've lost Clio, and those other dogs are yipping and yapping up on the lawn again. The girl turns back to look for me, and I give her a fleeting look that says, *Stay there*, though by now I know better, and I race after Clio.

When I get back out from under the dark trees and into the shade lighter of the sloping lawn, there's my damn mutt, digging. But in a different spot from earlier, when she turned out not to be the digger at all.

I can't see the man in the garden anymore. Clio's leash and glossy black fur are speckled with burrs, and one paw's swiping at something buried there—carefully, urgently. A clot of earth falls and breaks over the object, and then she's digging again to save her life, and to me the earth smells good and familiar because I'm a gardener, but now that man is upstairs in the window and I'm freaking out all over again.

JesusMaryandJoseph.

Another man, older and mean-looking, dressed in red like some kind of king without a crown and thoughtfully fingering his beard.

This place is crawling.

I get hold of Clio's leash and pull, but she won't have it; she snaps at me. She has her paw back on that hidden something, has almost eased it out of the earth like a favorite bone, and I see a piece of rotten fabric of some kind, wrapped around something glinting, something snared and shining-white even in this moonless place, this night that I now believe will never end, though it's barely begun.

The air smells like rain. I snatch up Clio's prize and slap her snout when she lunges. She relents, and I tug her to the gates. We enter the avenue and begin to run.

Those soldierly rows of trees are barely visible. Nothing is visible, really, though my eyes have adjusted a bit, and I seem to sense him before I see him. We're feet away when I make him out, the old man from the house, a ghastly, powerful-looking old king riding toward me on a monstrous huge horse that takes up the roadway. It's so dark that I can hardly make them out, but I hear the hooves on the gravel just in time. Clio's already ripped free again and we both veer into the trees, and it's a labyrinth, dark as pitch, and there are shapes sweeping past, weaving around us like gentle waves, waves Clio's size and smaller and one a good deal larger, though I barely make them out, snapping and yipping playfully—I hear that, too, remarkably, though I can't hear Clio breathing feet away—at my sweet dumb dog, who picks up speed as if to outdo them.

And there's the girl, a gleam in the wood, gesturing to us, and Clio runs toward her and so do I because I've lost my bearings, and Clio leaps over some brambles and lands . . . in the road.

The road.

But wait.

I look for the girl, and she's back there in the woods, smiling.

What a smile. When I'm an old guy playing poker in my wheelchair, I'll think of that smile and wonder. It's good to have a thing like that, like her—that you can't explain away. I smile back, the ripples settle, and my mind is like still water again. I push through the brush and scale that low stone wall Clio sailed right over, and step out into the road.

The lights of the village look to be a mile or so away as the crow flies. But I know better than to blunder through a bog. Clio does, too, so we find our pace with the windy heath beside. We stride toward the crossroads, where we'll find the road to those lights. White lights and red, coming and going lights, streetlights, pretty lights everywhere blurred by the sudden rain. A hard rain that instantly soaks my clothes and beads on Clio's glossy fur.

When I think to grope Clio's prize out of my pocket, the rain washes stinking scraps of fabric away, and I'm left holding the richest object I've ever seen, a pale blue pendant set in a soil-and-silver rope of diamonds.

I want to jump up and down in the fast-forming puddles. Call Da. Tell him we've finally hit the jackpot. But he'll only make me turn it in. There'll be fuss and paperwork.

Meanwhile, I have this crazy idea of going back for her, as if she were just some ordinary girl, just my high-school sweetheart in distress. I imagine leading her out of the dark wood by the hand, kissing her in the rain, presenting her with Clio's shiny find to watch how gems rest against that white, white throat. Sadness settles over me instead. I turn the piece over in my hands, and it's sharp. It's heavy. It's a glorified dog collar—a pretty noose—not something I'd weight Clio with, much less a girl who shines so well on her own.

She's gone now, anyway. They all are. I don't know how I know, but I do. I feel it in Clio's relaxed gait, in my own calm, in the fresh smell of the slowing rain. The woods are dripping-black and sleepy. I mumble a clumsy prayer and ask Mum to look for her, look after her, and we keep going through the waning storm. It isn't long before Clio, dumb mutt, is wagging her pink tongue and her tail, happily shaking off rain like diamonds, and I've never been glad to say this before, but I can't hear it falling. I can't hear a thing.

Acknowledgments

Edith Wharton's "Kerfol" is one of my favorite ghost stories. I originally set out to retell it, together with several other American gothic tales, but in the end my editors and I thought it might be more fun and original to really *inhabit* the story we liked best of the group—and the haunted house of its title. This book is the result.

In the first two stories, I worked in phrases and dialogue from the original, so this was at least in part a fortuitous (for me) collaboration with Edith Wharton.

Thanks to my editors, Liz Bicknell and Amy Ehrlich; to my agent, Jill Grinberg; to Katie Cunningham, Sherry Fatla, Kate Cunningham, Hannah Mahoney, Meghan Blosser, Amy Carlisle, and Audrey Brown; and to my dear friend and expert first reader, Lisa Goodfellow Bowe.

A Trio of Terrifying Tales

Gothic!
Ten Original Dark Tales

The Restless Dead
Ten Original Stories
of the Supernatural

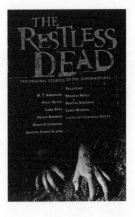

Sideshow
Ten Original Tales of
Freaks, Illusionists, and
Other Matters Odd and Magical

edited by DEBORAH NOYES with contributions from:

David Almond • M. T. Anderson • Holly Black •
Libba Bray • Neil Gaiman • Garth Nix •
And many more . . .

www.candlewick.com